The Ghost Rock Mystery

By Mary C. Jane

Cover by Gerald McCann

SCHOLASTIC BOOK SERVICES

NEW YORK • TORONTO • LONDON • AUCKLAND • SYDNEY • TOKYO

ISBN: 0-590-02513-9

Copyright © 1956 by Mary C. Jane. This edition is published by Scholastic Book Services, a division of Scholastic Magazines, Inc., by arrangement with J. B. Lippincott Company.

23 22 21 20 19 18 17 16 15 14 13 12 11   9/7 0 1 2 3/8

Printed in U.S.A.   11

The Ghost Rock Mystery

Other books by Mary C. Jane

MYSTERY IN OLD QUEBEC
MYSTERY AT SHADOW POND*
MYSTERY AT DEAD END FARM
MYSTERY BEHIND DARK WINDOWS

*Available from Scholastic Book Services

CONTENTS

To my favorite Vermonters

DOROTHY CANFIELD FISHER

and

JESSIE WHEELER FREEMAN

CHAPTER 1

The House in the Woods

When Janice saw the pink envelope in the mailbox her heart leaped joyfully. A letter on pink paper couldn't be from anyone else but Aunt Annabelle. She took it out of the box and glanced quickly at the handwriting. Yes, that was exactly what it was!

She hurried up the driveway to the house. It was always exciting to hear from Aunt Annabelle, for she and her eleven-year-old son, Hubert, were usually up to something. Janice wondered what it would be this time.

Her brother Tommy sat on the porch railing whittling on a miniature totem pole. He let out a whoop when he saw the pink envelope.

"A letter from Aunt Annabelle, Mamma!" he shouted, rushing into the kitchen ahead of Janice. "Hurry up and read it!"

Mr. and Mrs. Brooks had just finished lunch, and Mr. Brooks was getting ready to go back to work in the west field. He was a busy man at this time of year, with the planting to be finished and the haying begun, but he stopped short at Tommy's news and waited while Mrs. Brooks opened the letter.

There were several closely written pages, and she had not quite finished the first one when she gave a faint gasp, clapped her hand to her mouth, and murmured, "Oh, no!"

"What is it this time, Grace?" Dad asked. "Is Annabelle going to marry again? Or is she setting off on a trip to the African jungles?"

Usually Mother protested when Dad spoke like that about her sister Annabelle, but today she did not even notice. She just kept reading and looking more and more upset. When she came to the end she laid the letter down on the table and turned to Dad.

"Annabelle's bought a tourist home," she said.

"A tourist home," Dad repeated. "Why—that doesn't seem a bad idea. Annabelle might do well with a tourist home there in Portland."

Janice and Tommy felt let down. For once Aunt Annabelle had disappointed them. She was doing something so sensible and ordinary that even Dad approved of it. Why had the letter disturbed their mother?

Mrs. Brooks spoke again, more hesitantly. "That's just the trouble, Edwin. It *isn't* in Portland. Oh, dear," and she stopped to wipe her eyes on her apron, "it's away up in the wild woods. Here, read it for yourself!"

Dad took the letter and began reading as excitedly as Mother had done. As he read, the children saw his face grow grim.

"Well, that's really the limit," he snorted when he had finished. "A tourist home in the middle of the woods, almost in Canada! And she buys it because she says she gets more rooms for the money up there, and a gorgeous view. Great Gideon!"

"I don't think it's even *safe* for a woman alone, especially a young woman like Annabelle," Mrs. Brooks fretted. "It may be all right in the summertime, but what will she do in the winter? She'll have nobody but hunters and lumberjacks for neighbors."

"Well, there's nothing we can do about it," Dad said gloomily. "There never has been anything we could do about Annabelle's wild ideas. It's a pity John died, for if ever there was a woman who needed a sensible man to guide her, she's the one. I'm going back to work."

He went out, shutting the screen door behind him with so much extra firmness it was almost a bang.

"Don't feel bad, Mamma," Janice said comfortingly.

3

"It may not be so awful as you think. May Tommy and I read the letter?"

Their mother nodded, and the children raced through the pink pages. When they had finished their eyes were shining.

"Golly, Mamma, you didn't tell us she wants us to spend the summer with her and Hubert," Tommy cried.

"Can we go?" begged Janice. "We could help her get settled, and be company for Hubert, and—"

"Hubert!" Mrs. Brooks interrupted. "Don't talk about that boy to me. It's he who is responsible for this whole thing. It's because he liked the idea so much that Annabelle bought the place. She said so."

"But you've never seen it, Mamma," Tommy protested. "Aunt Annabelle says there is a lovely view of Boundary-Bald Mountain from her front porch, and sixteen rooms in the house, and it's not quite four miles beyond Jackman. It may be a wonderful place."

"Jackman is the jumping-off-place," Mrs. Brooks moaned. "It's a frontier town in the middle of a howling wilderness. Oh, if only Annabelle hadn't sold her nice little home in Portland. If only she'd rented this place and tried it out for a while, before she bought it!"

Tommy ran through the letter again, looking for more cheerful details.

"Her neighbors aren't lumberjacks," he declared.

4

"She says that her nearest neighbor is a member of the United States Border Patrol. I don't see what could be safer than having a policeman for a neighbor."

"Can't we please go, Mamma?" Janice pleaded again.

"It might be a help to Annabelle if you children were there for a while," Mrs. Brooks said, "and you could find out what the place is really like. If it's *too* bad your father and I will insist on their coming here with us until they can sell it and find something nearer home. We'll see if we can persuade Daddy that it's safe for you to go."

It took a good deal of talk and many letters back and forth between the Brooks' farm in southern Maine and Aunt Annabelle's new home before the matter was settled. At last, on the first day of July, Tommy and Janice set out by bus for their visit in what their father still insisted was the wild backwoods of Maine. For several hours they traveled through pretty towns and over pleasant highways.

When the bus stopped in a village called Caratunk, Tommy grumbled, "It doesn't seem like the wild woods to me."

"Did you think you'd see moose and bears beside the road?" Janice asked. "You have to get away from the highway for that."

A little later they passed through a place called The

5

Forks, and the bus driver explained that this was where the Dead River and the Kennebec met and became one stream. "It's the last town before Jackman," he added.

"How far is Jackman from here?" Janice asked.

"It's more than thirty miles, and nothing but woods all the way," the driver replied, adding with a grin, "You're entering God's country now."

Thirty miles of deep woods, with ever widening views of mountains and lakes, satisfied even Tommy's adventurous spirit. Through the open windows of the bus the smell of sun-warmed spruce and pine blew in.

"God's country," Tommy repeated, breathing deep.

As the bus came to a stop in Jackman, the children saw their cousin Hubert pointing excitedly toward them. Beside him stood Aunt Annabelle, looking like a wild rose, Janice thought, in a pretty pink dress.

"We've got a car," Hubert shouted, as they climbed down the steps of the bus. "Mom's learned to drive, and I'm learning, too."

Then they were hugged and kissed and exclaimed over by Aunt Annabelle while Hubert collected their bags and led the way to a very old green sedan parked near the post office.

"We had to have a car because Mountain View House is almost four miles out of town," their aunt explained. "So I bought this old relic, and learned to drive, and here we are!"

As she spoke, they piled into the sagging back seat, and the car started off with a jerk that tumbled their suitcases onto the floor.

"Hold onto your hats," Hubert warned them. "Mom's still a beginner at this."

"I'm a licensed driver," his mother declared indignantly. "It's not my fault if this old car won't start smoothly."

She drove at quite a speed, and they soon left the town behind. A long, deep-blue mountain loomed up ahead of them, and Aunt Annabelle said, "That's

Boundary-Bald. Isn't it beautiful? Your bedroom windows look right out on that."

Janice thought that it would be just like lovable, impractical Aunt Annabelle to give them the nicest bedrooms in the house.

"Shouldn't you save the rooms with the view of the mountain for the tourists who come?" she asked.

Aunt Annabelle laughed gaily. "Bless you, Janice, there's a view from every bedroom window in that house. We're in among the Boundary Mountains—Sally, and Burnt Jacket, and Granny's Cap, and a dozen other peaks are within sight of us. So we don't have to skimp on views. We've enough to go around."

A house with mountains and forests on every side could not help being exciting. Janice and Tommy sat on the edge of the seat staring eagerly ahead. Yet when the house actually came into view neither of them dreamed it was the right one until Hubert shouted, "There it is! That's Mountain View House!"

That gaunt, gloomy place—Aunt Annabelle's house? Tommy's eyes met Janice's and there was dismay in their gaze.

"If Daddy had even seen a picture of it, he'd never have let us come," he whispered, and Janice nodded agreement.

"It's awfully—big, Aunt Annabelle," she said, trying to sound admiring. "You'll have lots of room for tourists there."

Aunt Annabelle's laugh did not sound quite so merry as it had in other days. "We'll have room for them, all right, dear," she said, "if they'll just come."

"We've had only three so far," Hubert added, "and we've been waiting for two weeks."

The house stood on a long, bare ridge. A steep

10

driveway led up to it and made a semicircular sweep back to the road. It was a tall house with a square, overhanging third story that rested upon the house like the cover on an old-fashioned sugar bowl. The weather-worn paint might once have been dark gray but had now become almost earthen brown. Even the sign, MOUNTAIN VIEW HOUSE—TOURISTS ACCOMODATED, that swung from a branch of a big tree near the driveway needed new paint. The lettering on it was so faint it could hardly be read.

"We'll have a painting bee now that you children have arrived," Aunt Annabelle said. "We'll paint the window blinds and the front door a nice, gay yellow. And we'll make window boxes and fill them with geraniums and petunias. That will brighten the place up, don't you think?"

Janice and Tommy agreed that that would make it much more cheerful. But when they went into the house with its big, high-ceilinged rooms and dark halls and climbed to their rooms on the second floor they felt less and less sure that anything could be done to make it attractive to travelers.

"It just isn't cozy or homelike," Janice thought, "and I'm afraid it never will be."

Supper was not nearly as gay a meal as it usually was with Aunt Annabelle and Hubert.

"Are you worried because business has been dull?" Tommy asked.

Aunt Annabelle's eyes dimmed as if a cloud had

11

passed over them. "I'm worried about something," she admitted, "and I don't exactly know what. That's the worst of it."

Hubert had his mouth full of chocolate cake but he managed to splutter, "People around here don't seem to like this house. Or else they don't like *us*. Nobody ever comes here."

"The milkman won't even deliver milk to our door," Aunt Annabelle added. "He leaves it beside the mailbox. He says the driveway is too steep."

"I think maybe the house is haunted," Hubert gulped through another mouthful of cake. "But I don't care if it is. Now that you've come we'll have fun trying to find out what it's haunted *by!*"

Of course nobody really believed in ghosts or haunted houses. Yet Janice shivered and Tommy's honest gray eyes looked startled. The mountain shadows were already beginning to shroud the lawns outside the windows. The sign on the big tree at the foot of the drive creaked in a chill breeze that had sprung up. It was not hard to believe that something might be strangely wrong with this house in the backwoods. Perhaps this time Aunt Annabelle really had made a bad mistake.

CHAPTER 2

The Ghost in the Rock

The noise Hubert and Tommy made as they clattered down the stairs woke Janice early the next morning. Her room, that had felt so gloomy at night, was bright with sunshine now. White ruffles framed the windows, and the blue peaks of the Boundary Mountains looked down upon her with a peaceful beauty.

Aunt Annabelle called up the stairs, "Put on your old clothes, Janice. We're going to scrape paint this morning."

Janice caught a glimpse of herself in the mirror. In her pink pajamas she looked very much like her aunt. She had the same rosy coloring and dark hair, and the same dimples low in her cheeks. She thought she looked more like Aunt Annabelle's own child than her cousin Hubert did.

Hubert had a firm, straight mouth and dark eyes that looked at people a bit sharply. Grownups always thought he was a quiet, sensible child, and they never blamed him for anything that happened—unless they knew him very well, the way her mother and father did. Yet Janice knew he could think up more fun and mischief in a minute than Tommy would think of in a year.

"Tommy's *really* the sensible one," she thought, as she finished getting dressed. "But that short, freckled nose of his and those lively blue eyes make people think he's up to something all the time."

She hurried downstairs and joined the boys at the breakfast table in the kitchen, where they were gobbling pancakes. There were no long shadows to depress them this morning, and they were brimming over with cheerful plans.

"I'll clear up the dishes while you have a look around the place," Aunt Annabelle said. "Then we'll get together and start our painting."

They went outside, and Hubert showed them the empty barn and the remains of an old apple orchard. Beyond the orchard was a pasture partly overgrown with bushes and trees. Only the stone walls that ran along the edges of it and the big boulders that jutted out among the bushes made it clear that this had once been pasture land.

"Our property follows along the ridge," Hubert explained. "Below this ridge there is nothing but forest for miles and miles, clear into Canada. We aren't supposed to go into the woods unless we have a guide."

"I thought you had neighbors nearby," said Janice, almost frightened by the lonely wilderness before them.

"We have," Hubert declared, "but not very near. A man named Grant lives up the road about a quarter of a mile. The boy who drives the milk truck told me about him. He's a member of the United States Border Patrol. The men in the Border Patrol guard the land between us and Canada. They patrol all this wilderness, just like the Canadian Mounties."

"I'd like to meet him!" Tommy exclaimed.

"So would I," agreed Hubert. "I've been trying to think of some way to get acquainted."

When they got back to the house they found Aunt Annabelle standing in the driveway looking in dismay at the high third-story windows.

"We can never in the world get those blinds down to paint them," she said. "And what would be the use of painting the others and leaving them not done?"

"We'll have to get help, Mom," Hubert said quickly.

"We'll walk up the road and ask Mr. Grant if he could help us."

Aunt Annabelle was horrified.

"You mustn't do that," she cried. "What would he think—a perfect stranger like that—if we asked him to come and work for us? He isn't a handy man."

"Well," insisted Hubert, "we could ask him who we could get to help us. He must know who there is around here who does work like that."

Aunt Annabelle's eyes twinkled. "I see," she said. "You're looking for a chance to get acquainted with our Border Patrol man. Well, go ahead. We've got to meet him someday. I'll start taking the shutters off these downstairs windows while you're gone."

With a joyful whoop the three children scampered down the grassy bank to the road.

"It certainly isn't lonesome *here*." Janice laughed, as one car after another flashed past.

"This is the main highway to Quebec," Hubert said. "With so much traffic you'd think we'd get plenty of tourists at Mountain View House, wouldn't you?"

"It looks too dark and dreary," Tommy said frankly. "But when we get that yellow paint on the doors and blinds and window boxes it will make a big difference."

"I hope so," said Hubert. "Mom and I are worried. People have acted so queer about the house ever since

16

we got here. It makes us feel as if something must be wrong."

"Maybe, if Mr. Grant is friendly, we could ask him about it," Janice suggested.

They saw his house as soon as they rounded the curve. It was a neat gray cottage with a row of tall pines behind it.

"He lives all alone," said Hubert. "He's a bachelor, and I guess he likes to be by himself."

When they drew nearer the house they saw their neighbor splitting wood from a huge woodpile near the driveway. He was tall and strongly built, and had the lean, tanned face of an outdoorsman.

"He looks like a movie star!" Janice whispered delightedly.

Hubert and Tommy snorted at that. "He does not. He looks like a real man."

"Anyway," Janice murmured, "he looks just the way a Border Patrol man ought to look."

The friendly twinkle in his blue eyes made it easy to talk to him.

"So you're my new neighbors," he said, when they had introduced themselves. "I'm very glad to meet you. I'd been wondering who had had the courage to move into the old Totman place."

"Why did you think it took courage, Mr. Grant?" Janice asked quickly. "To move into that house, I mean?"

17

The young man shifted his glance so he did not have to meet their questioning eyes.

"Well—it's a big, old place, and pretty much run down," he explained. "And it's been empty for quite a few years."

Their faces showed that this explanation did not really satisfy them, and he went on lamely, "There have been foolish stories about the old house, as there usually are about big dark houses that have stood empty for years. No sensible person pays attention to such talk."

"Just the same," Hubert persisted, "we'd like to hear the stories. Then maybe we'd understand why people act so queer about our living there."

Mr. Grant smiled. "Well, perhaps I'll tell you—later. But why don't you tell me, first, whether you came on a special errand or just to pay me a call?"

They put their curiosity about the house aside and explained about the painting they planned to do and the trouble they had run into. Could he tell them who Aunt Annabelle could get for a job like that?

Mr. Grant said promptly, "How about me? I'd be glad to lend a hand. I'm off duty today and haven't anything important to do."

"Mom didn't think we should ask you to do it," Hubert said doubtfully.

"I'd like to," he insisted. "Let's walk back and see if your mother won't let me tackle the job."

As they started along the road he asked their names again. He was disappointed when Janice told him she and Tommy would only be there for the summer.

"I thought I was going to have a whole houseful of new neighbors," he said regretfully. "That's an awfully big place for only two."

"You said you'd tell us the stories people tell about our house," Hubert reminded him. "Will you do it now?"

Mr. Grant hesitated. "I'll tell you a little about it. But you must remember it's only a story. I wouldn't tell it if I didn't know you'd hear it from somebody else sooner or later. You seem to be sensible children who won't be scared by a lot of superstitious nonsense."

He paused, and Janice said hastily, "We don't believe in ghosts or haunted houses or things like that, if that's what you mean."

He gave them a serious, studying look.

"You don't believe in them with your minds, because you know they aren't real. But you do believe in them with your feelings? Do you get nervous when a door creaks at night or the wind howls around the house? Do you think of ghosts or such nonsense then? If you do, then you *half* believe in them, and even half believing can cause you a lot of trouble."

Janice remembered the strange feeling she had had at suppertime when the old sign creaked in the wind and the mountains cast their long shadows over the lawn. Did she half believe in ghosts?

Hubert declared, "Of course we don't get nervous about things like that. We're just worried because people act as if something was wrong with Mountain View House, and we're afraid it may spoil our tourist business."

"Well, let's see," Mr. Grant began. "The story goes back about sixty years, to a time when there were not many people living around here. This highway was only a dirt road and little used, for almost all travel was by train. There were very few houses on this road —my own house wasn't even built then, but yours was. It was just a farmhouse, not an inn or guesthouse then. A farmer named John Totman lived there with his wife and an elderly hired man. It was the hired man who first told this story.

"One cold, stormy night a traveler stopped at the house to ask for shelter. He was pale and sick, and his horse was ready to drop from exhaustion. But the Totmans refused to take the man in. They told him he'd find a tavern at Jackman, which was less than an hour's ride ahead. Next morning the stranger and his horse were found dead in a gully beside the road, hardly a stone's throw from the house."

Janice's eyes were dark with excitement, but the boys looked disappointed.

"Is that all?" Tommy asked. "I don't see why that story would frighten anybody."

Mr. Grant said with a laugh, "There's really nothing to it. Just because the Totmans were a hardhearted old couple who turned a sick stranger away is no reason to look upon them as murderers, or to believe there might be a curse upon their house forever afterward."

"A curse upon their house!" Hubert breathed. "Is that what people say about it?"

Janice felt the same inward chill that had fallen upon her spirits when the shadows had lengthened around the house. Yet she was sure she did not believe in ghosts or curses. She would not half believe in them either!

"We're not scared," she insisted. "Tell us what kind of things have happened at our house to make people believe there's a curse upon it."

Their neighbor smiled upon her approvingly.

"Good for you!" he said. "Well—the strangest thing that happened was the galloping sound of a horse's hoofs that was heard many times in a rock in the pasture behind your house. The Totmans' old hired man heard it first when he was burning juniper roots in the pasture one evening. It scared him so, he refused to stay on the place another day. Of course, he was an ignorant backwoodsman, and he believed

22

the sounds he heard in the rock were made by the ghost of the sick traveler and his horse."

"But who would believe him?" Tommy asked matter-of-factly. "Nobody else ever heard the ghost horse did they?"

Mr. Grant cleared his throat and looked a little uneasy. "Well—yes—they did. Quite a few people heard the hoofbeats in years past, or so they claimed. Some were very respectable people, too. Most of them are dead now, but people remember having heard them tell about it."

"Nobody's heard them lately, have they?" Hubert asked.

Mr. Grant shook his head. "Nobody in my day has ever heard them. Boys used to poke around the old pasture and listen beside all the big stones, but they could never find one that had any sound of hoofbeats in it. Nobody knows, any more, which rock it was that had once had the strange sounds within it."

They were almost in their own driveway now, and Mr. Grant stopped as if he had finished the story. But the children sensed that there was more.

"Something else must have happened," Janice said solemnly. "Something in recent years. People wouldn't be scared of the place today just because of that old ghost rock."

"Your mother will scalp me if I tell you anything

23

more," Mr. Grant protested. "I've told you the main part of the story. You can see that it's all nonsense, anyway."

"But you said respectable people heard the hoof-beats in the stone," Janice reminded him. "That part wasn't nonsense."

"Tell us what else happened, please," the boys begged. "If you don't, we'll ask the milkman and the mailman and everybody, until we find out."

Mr. Grant sighed. "I suppose you might as well hear it all. What happened was only a strange coincidence, but it made people who remembered the old story feel sure there really was something in it.

"A long time after the Totmans died, some people bought the house as an inn. It was when I was just a boy and I remember them well. They hung out that sign—MOUNTAIN VIEW HOUSE—and fixed up the place and hoped to do well taking summer guests.

"The first traveler to stop there was a wealthy man with a big car and a chauffeur. He stayed overnight. In the morning, when he started on his way, his car overturned and he was instantly killed. His chauffeur died the next day. He told the doctor, before he died, that he had lost control of the car because a stray horse had galloped into the road right in front of him."

"A stray horse," Tommy repeated in a whisper. "Did they find him—afterward?"

"No," Mr. Grant replied, "they never did find a

horse like the one the dying man described. And what made it so bad was that the accident happened in the very spot where the dead traveler and his horse had been found years before."

"Golly!" Hubert exclaimed. "No wonder people got scared."

"But we still don't believe it *means* anything, you know," Tommy declared stoutly.

"And we're not going to let it scare us," Janice added. "We'll find out the truth about that old horse if it takes us all summer!"

"You bet we will," agreed Hubert. "There must have been lots of horses around here in those days. There was no reason to think one stray horse was a ghost."

CHAPTER 3

Two Strange Visitors

They had been talking so excitedly that they did not hear Aunt Annabelle's voice calling them until they were almost at the door.

"Hubert—come here. Help me!"

"It's Mom!" Hubert cried.

"I see her," Mr. Grant exclaimed, starting down the hill at a run. "She's up in that maple tree!"

The children, being used to Aunt Annabelle's ways, were not surprised to see her stretched out at full length along a branch of the tree—the branch from which the sign—MOUNTAIN VIEW HOUSE—was suspended. The sign was hanging at a crazy angle while Aunt Annabelle clung wildly to the chain that had held it to the tree.

"Can you reach it?" she called down to Mr. Grant.

Tall as he was, he could not quite catch hold of the heavy sign.

"Can't you let it down just a few more inches?" he asked.

Aunt Annabelle groaned. "I'm afraid to let it move another inch. If I let go it might drop right down on your head."

"I'll risk it," Mr. Grant laughed. "You let it down and I'll be ready to catch it."

Hubert began to scramble up the tree.

"Wait a minute, Mom," he shouted. "Don't let that chain go yet. I'll come and help you."

"You can't get out on this branch, too, Hubert," his mother gasped. "Go back! Ouch! Oh, mercy—!"

She shrieked, Hubert slipped, and the heavy signboard dropped, all in the same second. Mr. Grant caught the sign, but the weight of it toppled him over into the ditch with the heavy board on top of him. Hubert half fell and half slipped down the tree trunk and landed in the dust below, while from the branch Aunt Annabelle stared down at them, her dark eyes horrified.

Mr. Grant stared back at his extraordinary new neighbor. Then he began to chuckle, and finally he burst into roars of helpless laughter. Janice and Tommy, who had been dismayed at first, began laughing, too. Hubert picked himself up and joined in the laughter, rather sheepishly.

After a minute Aunt Annabelle climbed down. She straightened her hair and brushed the pieces of bark from her pink blouse and blue jeans, while Mr. Grant managed to push the signboard off his chest and get to his feet.

Aunt Annabelle blushed in confusion.

"I don't know what you must think of us, Mr. Grant," she apologized. "I was just going to take that sign down so we could paint it. I never dreamed it would be so heavy. The chain slipped, and I was afraid to let go of it."

They moved back toward the house, signboard, stepladder, and all, each one trying to explain something to the others as they went.

Mr. Grant was so businesslike and helpful that before they realized what was happening, Aunt Annabelle and Janice were stirring up yellow paint in the barn, Tommy was on the third floor helping to remove the shutters, and Hubert was splashing paint on the old signboard that had caused all the trouble.

When Aunt Annabelle went in the house to start lunch Janice and Hubert talked over the strange tale Mr. Grant had told them.

"We've got to go out to the pasture and hunt for that ghost rock," Hubert declared. "If we could hear the hoofbeats we might be able to discover what really causes them. It certainly couldn't be any such thing as the ghost of a dead horse."

Tommy and Mr. Grant staggered into the barn just then, carrying two pairs of shutters from which the paint was peeling badly.

"We're going to scrape them, and then you and Hubert can paint them, Janice," said Tommy. "We'll bring down the others, too. And Mr. Grant's going to stay for lunch. Isn't that nice?"

Hubert and Janice agreed heartily.

"We're going to have strawberry pie for dessert," Janice said. "Aunt Annabelle's an awfully good cook."

"I'll bet she is," Mr. Grant replied. "I think she's an amazing person myself."

He looked toward the house to make sure she was nowhere in sight. Then he said in a low voice, "And listen, kids. I don't think you'd better tell her any of those old stories about the house. I'm afraid it would worry her. What do you think?"

Hubert shook his head. "We won't tell her," he promised. "But she's suspicious already. And if she sets out to find out about something, she'll do it—I know her."

They worked hard until lunch time and had so much fun listening to the stories Mr. Grant told about his adventures in the woods that they would have been glad to go on working afterward. But Aunt Annabelle refused to let them.

"A hard morning's work is enough," she said. "And we don't want to take advantage of Mr. Grant's kindness. Now that he's helped us get the shutters down we can surely finish painting them ourselves."

"Well, if you won't let me help, I'll get back to my woodpile," their neighbor said. "But I'll come over next week and put those shutters back on the windows."

When the lunch dishes were cleared away the children saw their chance to look for the ghost rock. They hurried through the orchard to the ridge at the top of the pasture. Pasture hardly seemed the right name for it, for the grass was as tall as meadow grass and was full of daisies and the burnt-orange flower of the Indian paintbrush. Rocks of all shapes and sizes jutted out of the sloping hillside.

"Where shall we start?" Janice asked in bewilderment. "I forgot that the pasture stretched so far."

"I thought we'd start with the biggest ones," Hubert answered. "But I didn't realize nearly all of them were big."

Tommy had been whittling on his totem pole, and his mind worked busily.

"I think we should start with the rocks below the ridge at the far end of the pasture," he said, pointing with his jackknife.

"But they aren't as big as some of the others," objected Hubert. "Why should we start with them?"

"Mr. Grant said the old hired man who first heard the hoofbeats was burning juniper roots in the pasture when he heard them. And those rocks are surrounded by juniper."

"Say—that's a clever idea," Hubert approved. "You've got a real brain in your head, Tom."

"I can think better when I'm whittling," Tommy said modestly. "You ought to try it, Hubert."

"Maybe I will," his cousin agreed. "We've got to be doing something while we sit around on these rocks. We may have to stay beside each one for hours. There's no telling when the sound of the hoofbeats may come."

The boys ran down the slope toward the stones in the midst of the juniper, but Janice stayed at the top of the ridge.

"I choose this one!" she sang out, as she scrambled to the top of a flat gray boulder. "This is big enough so I can lie down on it if I want to."

The early afternoon sunshine was bright and peaceful over the countryside. Janice clasped her arms around her ankles and rested her chin on her knees as she waited, listening dreamily for sounds in the rock beneath her. The story Mr. Grant had told seemed as unreal as a fairy tale, here in the matter-of-fact sunshine. Nothing could be less ghostly than this rough gray stone, warmed by the sun.

The dark fir woods that began at the lower edge of the pasture and stretched like a green ocean toward the Boundary Mountains were much more mysterious. In the flickering sunlight and shade under the nearest trees Janice thought she saw something move. Was she imagining things, or had a shadow really flitted under the green branches? She drew in her breath sharply, wondering if there could be a moose or a bear or even a person watching them from the shelter of the underbrush.

The thought frightened her, and she saw that the pasture was really a lonely place. Perhaps it was more suited to ghostly happenings than she had believed.

"If I see that shadow again," she told herself with a shiver, "I'll climb right off this rock and tell Tommy and Hubert about it. Maybe it isn't a safe place for us here."

She watched intently for a few minutes, but nothing happened. She had begun to think she must have imagined that motion under the trees when suddenly, from the very spot she was watching, an enormous crow flew out into the sunshine. He flew straight toward her. As if he knew she had been watching him, he perched on a nearby stone and stared at her with an almost human glance of curiosity.

Janice could not help laughing. Here she had looked for a wild animal or even a thief escaping across the border, and all that appeared was an old black crow!

The bird did not understand her laughter. He cocked his head, and his bright eyes gazed at her. Then he opened his yellow bill and spoke. In strange, cawing tones he said something that sounded exactly like a string of words, and he looked at her as if he expected her to answer him.

Janice stared at the creature in amazement. Had he really been talking? She had not understood a word he had said, yet it certainly had sounded like human speech. Janice patted the gray rock invitingly.

"Come over here, Blackie," she coaxed. "Come on, boy."

He did not stir from his perch but opened his mouth and muttered some more hoarse words. It sounded as if he were saying, *"Marn-jay—Marn-jay—Marn-jay!"*

Then, with another flapping of wings, he sailed off over the tops of the big pine trees into the depths of the woods.

Janice stared after him openmouthed. Had he been trying to tell her something? She had heard of pet crows who could speak a few words, almost like parrots. But this bird hadn't said anything a person could understand. And if he lived in the middle of the wilderness he couldn't be a tame crow, could he?

"When I come out here tomorrow I'll bring some crumbs for Blackie," she resolved. "Maybe I could get him to talk enough so I could figure out what he was saying."

It was hard to stay quietly on one rock when nothing happened, and the pasture was so full of others that should be investigated. Tommy and Hubert grew restless before even an hour had passed. It was not going to be easy to find that ghost rock, or to prove that Mountain View House did not have a curse upon it. Maybe it was not even going to be fun.

"But we won't give up," Tommy said firmly, "no matter how long it takes."

Janice told them about the crow's strange visit. "What do you suppose he meant by saying '*Marn-jay —Marn-jay*' all the time?"

"Maybe you didn't hear him right," Hubert answered. "Golly, I hope he comes again. It would be fun to have a talking crow for a pet."

Late in the afternoon the sky began to cloud over, and it looked like rain, so they started back to the house. They were surprised again by the gaunt, dismal look of the place. With the shutters stripped from the windows, it appeared empty and abandoned.

"We'd better forget everything else until we get those shutters and window boxes painted," Janice declared, "Tourists will never stop here while it looks like this."

By suppertime the rain began coming down in earnest. Aunt Annabelle set the table in the dining room, a room so enormous it seemed to the children like a banquet hall in some old castle. There was a fancy droplight in a green glass shade over the table, but the corners were full of shadows.

"When we bought this place I thought it was wonderful to have such a big dining room," Aunt Annabelle remarked wistfully. "I thought we'd serve break-
fasts to our guests here, and we'd need lots of space.
But I guess a small one would have done just as
well for all the guests we have."

"Mr. Grant says the tourist season hasn't really got
started yet," Janice said comfortingly.

"But I have a feeling nobody likes this house," Aunt
Annabelle fretted, "and I wish I knew why."

The children flashed secret glances at each other,
thinking of Mr. Grant's story, but they said nothing.
They ate their gingerbread and cream in a silence that
was disturbed only by the swish of the rain against the
windows.

Suddenly a sharper sound broke the stillness—the
long-awaited sound of knocking at the front door.
Aunt Annabelle almost tipped her chair over in her
hurry to answer it, and the children stole along behind
her and peered curiously into the hall. Maybe the
storm had brought them luck, and guests had come at
last!

There was only one man at the door, however, instead of the carful of people they had hoped for.
When he stepped into the hall the children were startled by his unpleasant smile and his hard, sharp eyes
that stared furtively around.

"I would like a room on the top floor at the back of

the house," he said harshly. "I don't sleep well, so I like to be away from the rest of the household where it is quiet."

"I'm sorry," Aunt Annabelle answered, "but the rooms on the top floor are not ready for guests yet. We have some nice rooms at the back of the second floor. I'm sure you would find them quiet and comfortable."

The stranger's brief smile vanished, and he looked angry. "There is bound to be noise on the second floor when the family goes to bed. I would rather have a room on the top floor—even if it isn't fixed up for guests," he insisted.

Aunt Annabelle turned toward the door and spoke coldly. "I'm sorry I can't let you have a third-floor room. Perhaps you will find something to suit you in Jackman."

The stranger hesitated, but made no move to go. He smiled again, though his eyes remained hard.

"Oh, I do not wish to look elsewhere," he said hastily. "One of the back rooms on the second floor will have to do if I can't have the other. Will you show it to me, please?"

He picked up his bag and followed Aunt Annabelle up the stairs.

Janice turned to the boys. "I wish he had gone," she whispered. "He has a mean face, and I don't like him."

"I don't like him, either," admitted Tommy. "Especially when he turns on that smile."

They went back to their places at the table and tried to finish their dessert. After one mouthful Hubert laid his fork down and leaned across the table toward Tommy and Janice, his eyes wide.

"Say," he whispered, "how did that man know our house was a tourist house? There wasn't any sign on the maple tree—it's in the barn being painted. Why should he stop here when there's nothing to tell him we take guests here?"

The cousins stared at each other wordlessly. In spite of themselves they thought of Mr. Grant's story of a stranger who had stopped at this house on a stormy night so many years ago. Was there—could there possibly be—any connection between that stranger—and this one?

CHAPTER 4

Footsteps Overhead

Aunt Annabelle came downstairs alone, so the children knew the stranger must have decided to stay.

"We don't like that man, Mom," Hubert said. "He looks dangerous."

His mother laughed. "You've been seeing too many movies, Hubert. You can't tell whether a man's dangerous or not from his looks. Lots of nice people look like criminals."

Janice fixed her gaze upon her aunt and said slowly, "But why did he stop here? How did he know this was a tourist house? There isn't any sign outside, tonight, to tell him so."

Aunt Annabelle stared back at Janice for a moment with a startled look. Then her face cleared and she said, "Goodness, let's not get to imagining things! You actually made me feel nervous for a minute. I suppose the man—his name is Mr. Jarrett—has passed here plenty of times before tonight. Probably he remembered seeing our sign and thought this would be a good, quiet place to stay."

The children breathed a sigh of relief at that reasonable explanation, but they were glad the unpleasant Mr. Jarrett remained in his room instead of coming downstairs to spend the evening. Aunt Annabelle made fudge, and Hubert and Tommy played a long game of checkers at the kitchen table. Janice began a letter to her mother and father, telling them all about the trip she and Tommy had made.

She bit her pencil thoughtfully as she bent over her writing. Such a lot had happened! There was the exciting story Mr. Grant had told them about the dead traveler and his horse, only she could not tell Mamma and Daddy about that. She could tell them about Mr. Grant, though, and what a good neighbor he was for Aunt Annabelle.

She wrote a paragraph about him and another about the work they were doing painting the shutters. She told about spending the afternoon in the pasture and hearing the crow who seemed to talk yet could not be understood. But she did not say a word about hunting for the ghost rock, nor about the hard-eyed stranger who was spending the night at Mountain View House.

41

As she sealed the letter she felt a little bit guilty about the things she had left out. If Daddy ever dreamed about the house's having a curse upon it, or guessed how lonely it was, he would probably send for them to come home right away!

When it was bedtime the three children tiptoed up the stairs and went to their rooms without saying even a whispered good-night in the hall. Nobody wanted to wake Mr. Jarrett from the sleep he needed so badly.

Janice's bed squeaked a little when she turned over in it, and she tried hard to lie still. Mr. Jarrett's room was next to hers, and even a slight squeak might bother him. But it was hard to keep from turning over a few times before she settled down. The harder she tried, the wider awake she became. Even after Aunt Annabelle had come upstairs to bed she lay awake, dreamily going over the events of the day.

A faint sound that seemed to come from directly overhead made her eyes fly open suddenly in the darkness. She sat up and listened. Could it have been a footstep she had heard? Was someone walking around in the room right above hers?

The soft *pad, pad* repeated itself and was followed by a faint creaking noise. It sounded like footsteps, all right, and very stealthy ones. But Janice remembered how the stairs at home sometimes creaked when nobody was there. Old houses were drafty and noisy, especially at night. It was silly to be afraid of such sounds.

"This afternoon I thought a moving shadow was a bear or a moose in the woods," she reminded herself, "and it turned out to be only a crow. I said I'd never be afraid of a shadow again, and I won't. Or a creaking floor, either."

With that, Janice fell asleep.

In the morning she woke to a wet, gray world. The mountains were lost behind veils of rain. But there was a cheerful smell of coffee and bacon in the air, and she hurried to get dressed. She opened her door gently, in case Mr. Jarrett were still asleep, and she was about to tiptoe down the hall when a soft, brushing sound on the wall above her made her look up.

Someone was coming down the stairs from the third floor! From her door Janice could see a man's feet and dark trouser legs moving ever so cautiously down the top steps. She closed the door, except for a tiny crack, and watched. The man stepped on each stair very lightly, as if to test it for creaking noises, then came slowly on. As soon as he was halfway down, she could see that it was Mr. Jarrett. His sharp eyes peered over the railing, trying to make sure there was nobody around to see him. When he reached the hall he hurried past Janice's door to his own room and shut himself in.

All the strange feelings she had had the night be-

fore about this man returned in a flood. Was he connected somehow, with the mystery at Mountain View
House and all the queer things that happened to people who asked for shelter there? Her heart pounded
wildly and her eyes were like saucers as she hurried
down to the kitchen.

Aunt Annabelle stared at her.

"My goodness, Janice, what's the matter?" she asked.

Janice caught her breath and answered with a shaky laugh, "Oh—nothing. When I smelled the coffee and bacon away upstairs I thought I must be late for breakfast."

"Well, it wouldn't have mattered if you were a few minutes late, dear," her aunt assured her. "You needn't have rushed like that."

Mr. Jarrett came down shortly afterward. He left his key on the hall table, paid Aunt Annabelle, and went off with only a gruff word or two about stopping again when he was back this way.

Aunt Annabelle was full of plans for getting the paint job finished and the sign back on the tree.

"You won't mind painting shutters on a rainy day like this," she said gaily. "I'll go out to the barn with you and help you get started."

They put on raincoats and rubbers and trooped out to the barn. Aunt Annabelle helped them get the paint stirred up again and the brushes ready, then she hurried back to the house.

As soon as she was gone, Hubert and Tommy began talking excitedly.

"We heard somebody walking around up on the third floor last night," Tommy told Janice.

"At first we thought it was just the wind making the

45

floors creak," Hubert rushed on. "Then we heard some sharp noises that sounded as if someone were trying to pry a door or a drawer open. So we knew there really was somebody up there."

Tommy's eyes were bright with excitement. "We think it must have been Mr. Jarrett," he said. "Remember, how he insisted he wanted a room on the third floor? He must have been hunting for something up there."

"I don't believe he found anything," Janice declared, "because I saw him sneaking down the stairs from up there this morning, and he didn't have anything in his hands."

She told them what she had seen and how she, too, had heard the footsteps during the night.

"Maybe he only went up there to sleep," she concluded. "You know he said the slightest noise would wake him up. Maybe we disturbed him when we went to bed, and he went up there to be quiet."

"I think we ought to go up and have a look around, anyway," said Hubert. "Maybe we could find out what he was after."

They all agreed about that. When they went back to the house for lunch, quite weary from their morning's work, they were glad Aunt Annabelle said they had done enough for one day. She shooed them out of the kitchen as soon as lunch was over.

"Now we can search the top floor," Hubert whispered. "Come on!"

They went quickly but quietly up the two flights of stairs. There were five airy rooms on the third floor, but there wasn't much furniture in them and there were no curtains at the windows.

Janice went to the window of the little back room at the end of the hall. She felt as high above the ground as if she were in a tall tower.

"There must be a wonderful view from here when the sky is clear," she exclaimed. "I'd love to have this room myself."

"This isn't the room where the footsteps were," interrupted Tommy. "They were in the corner room, right over ours."

They went into that room. It was easy to search it because there was so little in it. The walls and windows were bare, the bed had only a mattress on it, and the dresser drawers were empty.

They turned the mattress over, took out all the dresser drawers and looked in them and behind them, and inspected the small closet.

"There's certainly nothing in this room," Hubert declared. "Not even a loose board to make the sharp, creaking sounds we heard."

They searched the room over Janice's bedroom. The floor boards there creaked a little in places, but there was no loose board that could have been pried up. The two front rooms had more furniture in them. It took longer to go through them thoroughly, but when they were done they had found nothing.

"That little room at the end of the hall is the only one left," sighed Tommy. "There's nothing but a bed and a chair in there. We already know that."

"We'd better search it just the same," said Hubert. "At least turn the mattress and look in the closet."

Janice opened the closet door while the boys lifted the mattress. This closet was long and narrow, and darker than the others. She squeezed into the farthest end of it and felt around in the corners. On one of the hooks her hand closed around some long, dangling leather straps. She lifted them from the hook and brought them out into the light.

"What in the world is this?" she asked.

As she spread the cracked leather pieces apart she saw that they were fastened together, and there was a piece of metal attached to them. The boys looked at the contraption curiously, and Hubert shook his head.

"That couldn't be what Mr. Jarrett was looking for," he said.

Tommy's cheeks suddenly grew pale. He dropped the strap he had been holding and stepped back.

"D-don't you know what that is?" he gasped. "It's a bridle—a horse's bridle. It's old and worn out, but it's a bridle just the same. What is it doing—here?"

Janice dropped the bridle, and the three of them stared down at it with frightened eyes.

"That story Mr. Grant told us *can't* be true," Hubert muttered. "Yet everything that happens makes it seem as if the ghosts of that dead traveler and his horse were still hanging around this house!"

CHAPTER 5

Trouble for the Border Patrol

The rain continued for the next three days and Mountain View House was darker and gloomier than ever. For hours on end the children discussed the mystery of Mr. Jarrett and the old bridle. Hubert still believed the ghost rock would give them a clue to the mystery, once they found it. But the rocks and grass in the pasture were dripping wet, and they couldn't hunt for it.

The rainy weather made a good time to scrape shutters and splash yellow paint on them. The children were glad to have a few days in which nothing exciting or frightening happened. They spent most of their time in the barn, painting and scraping until their arms were lame. Even the window boxes and lawn chairs received a buttercup-colored new coat.

They finished the last window box and chair on the third afternoon just as the rain stopped and the clouds began to lift.

"About time, too," Hubert groaned. "I'm lame all over."

Aunt Annabelle suggested a hot bath to take the kinks out of his muscles.

"After that, let's celebrate!" she said gaily. "Nobody will be stopping here tonight because we haven't got our sign up yet. This may be our last chance to be away in the evening. Let's have dinner in Jackman and go to the movies afterward."

"Oh, good!" Janice cried. "I'm so tired of rainy days and yellow paint. I'd love to go."

They got ready quickly and climbed into the old car.

"I've got to find a man to put up a light over our sign," Aunt Annabelle said as they started off. "I think I saw an electrician's sign on a house just beyond the church. Keep an eye out for it, everybody!"

They found the place on the outskirts of town, and drove into the yard. The young man who came to the door smiled pleasantly when Aunt Annabelle told him what she wanted.

"I'll come," he said readily. "Where is your house?"

"It's about four miles down this road," Aunt Annabelle said. "People around here call it the old Totman place."

The young man's mouth fell open and he stared at her curiously. Then he looked away.

"I'm sorry," he said, "but I have some work that must be finished tomorrow. If you go and see the boss at the hardware store he'll find someone to do it for you."

He stepped back inside the house and closed the door so quickly Aunt Annabelle didn't have time to protest.

She backed the car out of the yard, muttering angrily under her breath, "How can a grown man be so silly? You'd think he was afraid of Mountain View House!"

The children exchanged worried glances. Would this new happening make Aunt Annabelle ask questions that they could not answer without telling her the stories Mr. Grant had asked them not to tell?

A stream of late afternoon traffic kept her too busy for questions just then, however, and luckily the owner of the hardware store had a helper who agreed to come out to their house and install the light. After that, Aunt Annabelle seemed to have put the thought of the other man's strange behavior out of her mind.

They left the car in front of the store and scurried about doing errands that had been put off during the rainy days. Janice enjoyed walking up and down the wide street past the many stores and hotels. She liked to gaze up at the circle of blue mountains that surrounded the town, and to catch a glimpse, between the stores, of Big Woods Lake whose waters stretched back for miles into forests no roads or railroad tracks could reach.

"Jackman seems like a real frontier town," she said happily. "It makes me feel adventurous."

Hubert spoke up excitedly. "It looks more like a Western movie every minute. Look!"

He pointed toward the post office. There, striding along the sidewalk, was a tall man in a dark green uniform and cap. He wore a heavy black gun belt and leather shoulder strap, and he walked with the same free swing of many a western movie hero. As he came nearer they felt something familiar about him, and suddenly Tommy shouted, "It's Mr. Grant!"

The children raced toward him.

"Golly, Mr. Grant, I didn't know the men in our Border Patrol wore *uniforms*," Hubert exclaimed.

"It's like the Canadian Mounties—only *better!*" Janice breathed.

"Huh," Hubert scoffed, "she's never seen a Canadian Mountie, so how would she know?"

"Well, I've seen pictures of them," Janice defended herself, "and I think they're wonderful. But I always thought it was kind of silly to wear those bright red jackets and big, wide hats in the woods. A criminal

53

could see them coming a mile away. This Border Patrol uniform is just right for not being seen in the woods and it's just as handsome, too!"

Aunt Annabelle had come up in time to hear Janice's words, and she spoke up before the boys could make any teasing remarks.

"I agree with Janice," she said. "The Canadian Mounted Police are wonderful, but I think it's time people realized the United States Border Patrol is wonderful, too."

"Well!" Mr. Grant exclaimed, grinning, "I hardly know what to say to all this. I ought to say, in justice to our friends across the border, that they don't always wear those red coats and wide hats. Those are really their dress uniforms. In the woods they wear plain working clothes the same as we do. But I'm certainly glad you think our Border Patrol uniforms look just as good. . . . I was going to stop at your house after supper," he told them, after a minute. "I have to drive to the customs office at the border tonight and I thought you might like to go along."

"Oh, yes!" the children cried. "We'd lots rather do that than go to the movies!"

"After the sign goes up again I'll have to stay home evenings, in hopes some tourists will stop," Aunt Annabelle explained. "So tonight seemed our last chance for a fling."

Mr. Grant joined them for supper at the restaurant, and they had a merry time. The boys were full of questions.

"Do you patrol the woods over the mountains and everything between here and Canada?" they asked.

Mr. Grant told them about the Border Patrol camp twenty miles from town in the middle of the forest.

"Two of us at a time take turns staying there to inspect lumber camps and patrol the woods," he explained. "And that reminds me: my turn at camp comes up next week and I won't be able to come over to help with those shutters. Since you've finished the painting, couldn't I stop in tomorrow night and help get everything back in place?"

Aunt Annabelle said that would be fine.

Tommy had been trying to get up courage to ask a very important question, and he finally got it out.

"Mr. Grant, is the Border Patrol a part of the FBI?"

Mr. Grant laughed and shook his head. "No, we're not, Tommy. Our patrol comes under the direction of the Federal Bureau of Immigration. If you took the first letters of those words you'd get FBI, wouldn't you? But it's not the same."

"Why not?" Tommy asked.

"Well—the FBI that you mean is the Federal Bureau of Investigation. The men who belong to that track down national and international criminals and spies. But the Bureau of Immigration is different. They decide about letting people from other countries come into the United States."

"And the Border Patrol has to protect our country's borders and keep people out if they aren't supposed to be here?" asked Tommy.

Mr. Grant was pleased to see how quickly he understood.

"That's right. If you lived in Texas or Arizona you'd hear lots more about the Border Patrol than you do here. Down there, workers are always trying to swim across the Rio Grande and slip into our country. The

56

Border Patrol has caught thousands of these 'wet-backs,' as they call them."

"But why can't they come into our country?" asked Janice.

"Many of them could," Mr. Grant replied, "if they would go about it as they are supposed to do. If they sneak in, we never know how many men among the ordinary laborers may be dangerous enemies who are using this way to get into the United States. Sometimes there are people from Europe who can't get permission to enter our country, but they can enter Mexico or Canada. Then they try to slip across our border. There are men here who will help them get across if they are paid a high price. It's this kind of smuggling that the Border Patrol has to be on the watch for."

He was silent for a minute or two, and his face was serious. At last he said, in a worried voice, "We're having that kind of trouble now—right here. For a year or more, large numbers of aliens have been getting into our country from Europe. They enter Canada and then get across the border by some means we can't discover. The federal agents are pretty sure that they're entering in our area, so naturally we officers here are worried. We're doing everything we can, but so far we have no idea how they are getting through."

"It sure is an exciting job," Tommy said admiringly. "I'd like to be in the Border Patrol when I grow up."

"Maybe Mr. Grant will tell us about some of his adventures while we are on our way to the customs office," Aunt Annabelle said. "I'll drive back home and meet you all there."

When Aunt Annabelle had parked the old car in the yard at Mountain View House and they were all together on the way to the customs office, the children begged Mr. Grant to tell some stories about his adventures.

"You ought to be with us in the woods in winter when the snow is nearly up to our waists," he said. "You'd realize there's as much plain hard work as there is adventure to this job."

"I should think you'd get terribly tired patrolling the wilderness in winter," Janice sympathized.

"Oh, there's lots of fun, too," Mr. Grant admitted. "We have a snowmobile to get us around a good deal of the time, through the woods roads. It has skis in front and an engine in back, and it has round windows. You ought to see us travel in that!"

He told them stories of meeting bears and moose in the middle of the night, of losing his shoes in a river he waded across, and having to buy some horrible old ones from a lumberjack for a terribly high price, and of many other amusing experiences.

They traveled through miles of woods, past beautiful mountains and streams, with hardly a sign of civilization except for a gas station or two. The customs office seemed to be located in the middle of the wil-

derness. Mr. Grant went in to talk with one of the officers while Aunt Annabelle and the children sat outside and watched another customs officer examine the papers and the cars of people who stopped there on their way back into the United States.

A clear, peach-colored sunset tinted the sky above the mountains, and the spruce trees cast long, dark shadows across the road. Mr. Grant came out after a few minutes and said, "Let's drive on to the Canadian customs house. I'll speak to the officers there, and they'll let you walk over the line into Canada a ways."

He drove fast, because the dusk was deepening. Once or twice he slowed down as they passed a cleared field, and showed them several deer feeding near the edge of the woods.

"They always come out just before dark," he said.

The children watched with fascinated eyes. At last they were really in the heart of this wilderness, even though they were on a highway!

They walked over the border into Canada, as Mr. Grant had promised. The dark fir woods closed them in on either side, and only a faint glow of the peach-colored light was left in the sky.

"We're in Canada!" Janice breathed, half aloud. "I just can't believe it."

To herself she thought, as they traveled homeward through the darkness, "It's a strange, beautiful country but it's lonely and dangerous, too. I'm awfully glad Mr. Grant lives near!"

CHAPTER 6

The Secret on the Top Floor

Thursday was a bright, breezy day, and a lively one at Mountain View House. The electrician arrived early to fix the light over the sign. He was not the least bit afraid of the house, but bustled in and out, whistling as he worked.

Aunt Annabelle was busy, too, stitching up new bedspreads and curtains for the rooms on the top floor.

She asked the children to weed the flower beds along the driveway, and they worked at it all morning.

"On a day like this it seems silly to worry about Mr. Jarrett or that old bridle we found in the closet," Tommy said.

"I know it," Hubert admitted. "We shouldn't have

been so scared about it. I suppose someone might have left it there years ago and forgotten it."

"A bedroom closet is a queer place to leave a horse's bridle, though," mused Janice. "And Mr. Jarrett had no business going up there and sneaking down the way he did."

"Whatever he was up to, I don't believe it had anything to do with the old stories about the house," Hubert declared. "We wouldn't have been frightened when we found the bridle if we hadn't remembered the dead traveler and his horse."

"Maybe Mr. Jarrett is one of those smugglers who are helping foreigners get across the border," Tommy suggested in a scared voice.

The children set down their weeding tools and looked at each other.

"Do you suppose he could be a smuggler?" Janice faltered.

Hubert thought for a minute. "There's one thing we never did find out about him," he said. "We got so scared when we found the bridle that we forgot all about the sharp, prying sounds Tommy and I heard in the night. We never discovered what had made that noise."

"We ran away like cowards," Tommy remembered ruefully. "We'd better not let Mr. Grant know about it. If he knew those old stories he told us had made us afraid of our shadows, he'd never tell us anything again."

"We'd better not tell Mom, either," said Hubert. "She might decide to sell this house and move back to Portland if she thought there was any real danger here. And I want to stay."

They stopped talking for a minute and looked around them at the clear blue of the windswept sky and the deeper blue of Boundary-Bald and Burnt Jacket and the many other mountains. They breathed deeply of the morning air that was sweet with balsam and pine and the earthy smell of the garden they were weeding. They looked at Mountain View House, big and dark and a bit gloomy just now, but full of secrets that promised adventure. Oh, they all wanted to stay!

"We should have looked for a loose board in the walls or the floors," said Tommy. "Those sounds we heard must have been made by something wooden being pried up."

"Let's hurry and get this job done," muttered Hubert, tossing a handful of weeds over his shoulder. "Then we can search up there again."

They began pulling the weeds with great speed, but though they finished the work early, they did not get a chance to slip up to the top floor. Aunt Annabelle wanted to take the window boxes to town to have them filled with geraniums and ivy, and she needed them to help her. While they were in Jackman they stopped for a swim in Big Woods Lake, and this made them late for lunch. After lunch Aunt Annabelle went up to the third floor herself, to measure and fit the new curtains and bedspreads, so the children could not do any searching up there then.

"Let's go out to the pasture," said Hubert. "The ghost rock is more important than that queer Mr. Jarrett, anyway."

As they walked along toward the ridge Janice said thoughtfully, "I don't think there could be *two* mysteries about Mountain View House. If Mr. Jarrett has a secret reason for stopping here, it must be connected with the other mystery somehow."

They spent the rest of the afternoon in the pasture, listening hopefully beside several different rocks. This time Hubert and Janice had books to read and Tommy had his whittling, so the time passed pleasantly. But no sound came from the quiet old rocks, and not even Blackie came to disturb the stillness. By suppertime Janice and Hubert were quite discouraged.

"Finding the rock is only the start in solving the mystery," Hubert complained. "If we can't find it, we can't get started. We'll never be able to figure things out."

"We shouldn't expect to find it right off," Tommy declared stubbornly. "You heard Mr. Grant say that boys had hunted around this field for years, when he was young, and never found it. I bet even Sherlock Holmes didn't solve mysteries in a couple of days."

Aunt Annabelle had a picnic supper waiting for them out on the porch, and before they finished eating, Mr. Grant arrived.

"All ready to go to work on those shutters?" he asked, seating himself on the steps.

"You bet!" answered Hubert. "We can't wait to see how the house will look with the sign lighted up and the windows fixed."

"I've got a favor to ask of you," Mr. Grant said. "I have to leave for the Border Patrol camp in the morning, and my friend Bill Stickney, who usually looks after my hens when I'm away, is sick. I wondered if you'd be willing to feed and water the hens for me and collect the eggs, while I'm gone?"

"They'd love to," Aunt Annabelle assured him. "They'll be delighted to have a chance to do something for you, you've been so good to us."

They went out to the barn to begin work while Aunt Annabelle cleared the supper things away.

"You can handle these second-floor shutters, Hubert," Mr. Grant said. "Just carry them up and leave two in each room. Tommy, you take the third-floor pile. Janice can help me with the downstairs windows, and then I'll come up and help you boys with the others."

Tommy's heart skipped a beat at Mr. Grant's words.

The third-floor shutters! They had not been up to that floor since they had found the bridle in the closet. There were not as many shutters to go up to the third floor, since there were not as many windows. Maybe, if he hurried, he might find a few minutes to look around up there for a loose board in the floor, before Mr. Grant came up to help.

He started quickly into the house and up the stairs. As he worked, his mind went back to the night of Mr. Jarrett's visit. That prying sound he and Hubert had heard had been right above their own heads. It *must* have been in the back corner bedroom directly over his own.

"This time I'm going to examine every floor board in that room," he told himself.

He laid the first pair of shutters in the small back room and hurried down for more. He worked so fast he was out of breath before he finished, and even then he was not very much ahead of the others. When he laid the last pair of shutters in the front bedroom he almost ran to the corner room he had decided to search. He dropped to his knees and began creeping from wall to wall, looking each board over carefully for some sign of scraped wood where a knife or a chisel might have been used to pry it up. He crawled under the bed and moved the dresser to one side so as not to miss a single board. Yet when he reached the farthest corner he had not found a thing.

Then he remembered the closet. He had not examined that. It was so dark in there he could not see what he was doing, but he moved his hands over the separate boards carefully. Was that a raised edge his fingers felt, in the far end of the closet? He pressed hard against it and felt it give slightly under the pressure. With a thumping heart he jumped up. He must find a knife and try to pry that board up—a knife and a flashlight so he could see what was there.

He was rushing toward the stairs when he heard voices. Hubert and Mr. Grant were starting up to help him.

"All set to hang those last shutters!" Mr. Grant announced.

Tommy tried hard to stifle his impatience. The loose board would have to wait. When the work was done they would come up and explore the secret place together. But the top-floor shutters were the hardest ones to hang, and it seemed to take hours before they were finished. Then there were still the window boxes to attach to the downstairs windows.

When everything was finally done, Aunt Annabelle turned the light on over the newly painted sign, and they all walked up the road a way to see how Mountain View House looked in its new splendor. They exclaimed with delight when they saw the change their work had made. The new sign was as gay as a dancing buttercup, and the house had a friendly and welcoming air.

The children went on up the road with Mr. Grant. He wanted to show them where the food for his hens was kept and explain about taking care of them. But Aunt Annabelle went back to the house.

"Guests might stop any minute, the way it looks tonight," she said happily.

It was almost dark when the children started back from Mr. Grant's house. A strong wind had come up and was tossing the branches of the trees along the way.

"I hope it isn't going to rain again," Janice groaned.

"Never mind that," said Tommy. "We've got something important to do, rain or no rain."

He told them what he had found in the closet of the corner room, and they started running in their haste to get home and find out if there really was something hidden under that loose board.

They found a big car parked in the yard, and Aunt Annabelle met them at the door with a warning Sh—sh!

"We've got four ladies from Boston in our two best bedrooms!" she told them in a low voice. "They're returning from a trip to Quebec and they're tired. We must be very quiet. Think of it—four guests at once!"

She was so pleased she did not notice that they were silent, absorbed in thoughts of their own. She went out to the kitchen to get things all ready for an early breakfast, and the children hurried up the stairs like flying shadows.

Tommy got his jackknife and flashlight from his room, and they stole on up the second flight of stairs to the corner room. There was not enough space for them all in the narrow closet, so Tommy crawled in on his hands and knees and the others peered in from the doorway.

"It really is loose!" Tommy whispered. "There are scraped places, too—you can tell it's been pried up."

He dug at the board with his knife while Hubert and Janice watched breathlessly. Each time the board squeaked and creaked he had to stop and try to ease it up more slowly. They must not disturb the guests on the floor beneath, no matter what.

"It's lucky they've got the front rooms," Janice murmured. "I don't think they can hear us from there."

The board came up at last, and under it lay a neat cubbyhole, quite free of dust and cobwebs, and holding—to the children's astonishment—nothing at all but a big, shining flashlight three times the size of Tommy's own. No money, no secret maps or papers, nothing the least bit mysterious.

Tommy lifted the flashlight out, and he and Hubert examined it with puzzled eyes, but Janice turned away, frowning. She had felt so sure this secret hiding place would hold some clue to the strange secret of the house that she could not help being disappointed. What could a common thing like a flashlight have to do with a mystery that involved a dead traveler and his horse and ghostly hoofbeats from long ago?

"Every time I think something really exciting and important is going to happen, it turns out to be something simple," she said disgustedly. "Just like seeing a crow when I expected to see a moose."

Tommy, as usual, looked at this new discovery with stubborn cheerfulness.

"Maybe the flashlight isn't a clue to the mystery," he said, "but it proves Mr. Jarrett was up to something. Maybe he keeps this light hidden here so he can hunt for some secret thing *he* knows about."

"He said he'd be back," whispered Hubert. "Let's leave the flashlight here and see what happens next time he comes."

They laid it back in the dark cubbyhole, and Tommy pressed the loose board into place. They went downstairs in perplexed silence. Would they ever find the answers to all the queer things that happened here at Mountain View House?

CHAPTER 7

The Storm

Remember now—no noise!" Aunt Annabelle cautioned them, when they had said good night. "We want these ladies to be pleased with our house so they'll tell others about it."

The children crept silently upstairs, but as Janice undressed in her room she was startled to hear the wild noise the wind was making. It howled around her windows and set the shutters and windowpanes to rattling.

It didn't seem as if she had been asleep very long when a loud banging sound wakened her. The wind's howl had risen to a wild shriek around the windows, and the banging was repeated again and again.

One of the newly painted shutters must have come loose, she realized in dismay. Could she possibly fix it? If she did not, the banging might wake everyone

in the house. The shutter might be ruined, too. But if
she opened the window in such an awful wind, who
knew what might happen?

Janice opened the window cautiously and was re-
lieved to find that the wind did not blow into her
room, though it was whirling madly past the window.
She caught hold of the swinging shutter and leaned
out to feel for the hook that should hold it, but it was
beyond her reach.

She had helped to hang several of the shutters and
she knew how they were fastened They were only

hooked at the bottom. If she lifted this one up, the little bolt at the top would slip out of its holder, and the shutter would be entirely out of its fastenings. She would be able to bring it right into her room, and let it stay here until morning.

In less than a minute she had followed out her plan and had set the heavy shutter on the floor. She started to close the window when, to her startled surprise, she saw a light—a smoky, orange-colored light like the flame of an old-fashioned kerosene lantern—moving along the road toward Mountain View House.

As her eyes grew accustomed to the darkness she saw, in the murky glow of the lantern, the silhouette of the person who was carrying it. It was a man, bent and slow-moving as if he might be very old. He had a cap on his head and was wearing a loose coat that billowed around him in the wind.

What on earth was an old man like that doing, walking the highway in the middle of a stormy night? Janice watched until he passed out of her sight toward the front of the house where he could not be seen from her window.

She stood there a moment thinking about the strange happening, when with a gasp of surprise she saw the same light and the same bent figure moving slowly up the driveway almost under her window!

Too astonished to move, she stood and watched while the old man, an odd black image in the smoky light of his lantern, moved slowly toward the barn.

"He must be a tramp," she told herself. "Probably he thinks there's hay in the barn and he's looking for a place to sleep. I'd better tell Aunt Annabelle."

She waited another minute, wondering how to wake her aunt without making noise that would arouse the guests in the house. Her eyes still followed the moving light. All at once she realized that it had gone past the barn. It was only dimly to be seen, moving on through the trees of the apple orchard.

It was then that Janice began to be afraid. This was no tramp looking for a place to sleep! Neither would any other ordinary person be wandering through their yard and orchard and on to the pasture ridge, at midnight of a stormy night. A chill began to creep up her spine to the very roots of her hair. Without waiting to let herself think about what it could mean, she fled across the hall to the room where Tommy and Hubert were sleeping.

"Wake up!" she whispered, shaking Tommy's shoulder. "Wake up!"

Even in their surprise at being aroused so strangely, both boys remembered the need of silence and they spoke in whispers.

"What's the matter?"

Janice told them what had happened, and they hurried back to her room.

The light had disappeared over the ridge when they reached the window. There was nothing but blackness and the howl of the wind outside now.

"Are you sure you weren't dreaming?" Hubert asked.

Janice pointed to the shutter on the floor and told them how she had had to unfasten it and take it inside to stop its banging.

"If she was wide awake enough to do that, I guess she couldn't have been dreaming," Tommy said.

75

"I think we ought to tell Aunt Annabelle," Janice whispered shakily.

Hubert protested, "She'd be upset if we woke those ladies, and anyway, what could Mom do? Let's watch from the window for a while and see if the old man comes back."

Until now the storm had been only a windstorm, but as they waited, kneeling by the window in the darkness, the rain began to beat upon the glass, hurled against it in sudden gusts by the wind.

"What can an old man do out on the ridge in this rain?" Hubert demanded. "He must be crazy."

"I began to wonder if it really *was* a man—even though I saw him," Janice breathed with a shiver.

"Do you mean you think you were dreaming, or having a nightmare?" Tommy asked.

"I mean—maybe he wasn't—real. Maybe people really do—see things—here at Mountain View House," Janice whispered.

The other two stiffened at her words, and she added faintly, "He looked to me—like the ghost—of the Totmans' old hired man. Who else would carry a lantern out to our pasture at midnight on a night like this?"

"Mr. Grant would be sorry he ever told us that story, if he could hear you now," Tommy scolded. "You *know* there are no such things as ghosts—really."

Hubert sniffed. "That's a girl for you! One minute they tell you they don't believe in ghosts—'Oh, goodness no, not at all!'—and the next minute they see an old man with a lantern and tell you they don't think he's real!"

Janice was too upset to try to defend herself.

"You didn't see him," she whispered.

Tommy and Hubert consulted together in whispers. They concluded that Janice had had a kind of nightmare that made her think the old man and his lantern had gone over the ridge to the pasture.

Hubert yawned. "We'd better get back to bed, Tom."

Janice knew they thought she was being silly, but she protested stubbornly. "If you leave me here alone I'll go wake Aunt Annabelle. You've got to stay with me at least a little while. He might—come back."

In spite of their sleepiness and their disbelief in Janice's "ghost," the boys agreed to stay a few minutes longer. They huddled together in the darkness and waited. Five minutes passed so slowly it seemed like an hour, and Hubert declared he would fall asleep on the floor if they stayed any longer.

Suddenly Janice whispered, "Look!"

Over the pasture ridge the smoky light reappeared and moved slowly toward them through the orchard. On past the barn it came, until it was near enough so they could see the old man, his head bent lower than ever against the rain, his lantern swinging in his hand.

Nobody said a word. They held their breath in dumfounded silence until they had to let it out in loud sighs.

The strange figure disappeared from sight for a few minutes, then they saw the light again, moving along the road toward town.

"It isn't a ghost," Hubert insisted, through chattering teeth. "There are n-no such things as g-ghosts."

But if it wasn't a ghost, what was it? That was the question that disturbed them so that they could not shake off their fright.

"He went right over the ridge—toward the ghost rock," Janice repeated. "M-maybe he—or s-somebody —doesn't like to have us hunt around that pasture so much."

"Just remember that *we don't believe in ghosts,*" Tommy comforted her. "If you remember that, you'll be all right. Whoever the old man was, he's gone now. And the storm is dying down, too. By morning we may be able to figure out what this was all about. So let's go back to bed."

Janice let them go this time. As she snuggled down in her blankets she reminded herself sleepily, "Mr. Grant said we shouldn't even half believe in ghosts, and he ought to know. But who could that old man have been?"

CHAPTER 8

Blackie Again

When Janice woke up the next morning her heart was heavy. For the first time, she began to feel that something weird and wrong really did hang over Mountain View House.

"If only Mr. Grant weren't going away," she thought, "it wouldn't seem so bad."

If they could have told him about the ghostly old man with the lantern, he might have known what to do. With him gone, whom could they turn to?

Outside her window the sunshine glittered on the wet leaves and grass. Clouds of mist were lifting slowly from the deepest hollows of Boundary-Bald, and Sally Mountain, Burnt Jacket, and Granny's Cap were sharply blue against the morning sky. But all the blue brightness could not make her forget the midnight visitor who had looked so much like the old hired man in Mr. Grant's story.

"I told him I didn't believe in ghosts—and I didn't," she whispered, "but I hadn't seen one—then."

Down in the kitchen Aunt Annabelle was bustling cheerfully about, getting breakfast for their guests. She was too busy to notice Janice's heavyheartedness or the unusual quietness of the boys. When the ladies came down to breakfast they declared that Mountain View House was just about the nicest place they had stayed on their whole trip. They went out on the front porch and exclaimed again and again about the wonderful air and the wonderful view.

"I think we've got a start, at last," Aunt Annabelle said happily, as they drove away.

Janice and the boys looked at each other and said nothing. It would be better if she did not know that there was—something—that did not like having people fix up the old house or hunt for the ghost rock.

Hubert and Tommy set to work mowing the wide lawn, while Janice helped clean up the kitchen and do over the guest rooms. When they had finished their work and found a chance to talk together it was almost noon. They stretched out in the comfortable lawn chairs, while Aunt Annabelle went back to the kitchen to bake muffins.

"Shall we tell her?" Janice asked abruptly. "It seems as if she should know about that old man."

"We can't," Hubert declared. "She'd be so upset I don't know what she might do."

Tommy said thoughtfully, "Mr. Grant will be back in a few days. Couldn't we wait until we talk with him? He's lived here all his life, and he doesn't think there's anything wrong with Mountain View House."

Hubert nodded. "It must have been just about midnight when that old man appeared. If he should come back, he'd probably come at that same time. We could watch for him, and if we saw him again we'd tell Mom about it."

Having a plan to follow was a relief. Their spirits lifted a little, and they decided to go out to the ridge and have a look around. They hoped the old man might have left something behind that would give them a clue to who he was, or at least prove that he was *real*. But the pasture was exactly as it had always been. The air smelled sweeter than ever and the gray rocks were warm with sunshine. There was not a clue to show that anyone had visited the place at midnight.

"Maybe we should stop hunting for the ghost rock," said Janice. "Now that the house is fixed up and people have started coming, maybe we should forget about those old stories."

Hubert protested at that. "It's easy for you to say. You and Tommy will be going home in September, but I'll still be here. When I'm at school, Mom will be all alone. I want to prove that there isn't any curse on this house."

"I don't see how it will help if we hear the hoofbeats," said Janice. "Won't that be just one more proof that the house *is* haunted? Won't it be one more scary thing, like Mr. Jarrett's footsteps and the old man with his lantern?"

Hubert shook his head. "If we hear them we'll have something to start on. The ghost rock is the only part of those old stories that we can do anything about. If we really heard the hoofbeats, I bet Mr. Grant would help us find out what is causing the sound. Then we could prove that those other things that happened— like the man and his chauffeur who got killed—were just accidents and had nothing to do with our house."

"We need to find some very old person who can remember farther back than Mr. Grant can," said Tommy. "There must be a few people still living around here who could tell us which rock it was supposed to be."

Janice was silent. For a long time now she had been thinking that the best time to hear the hoofbeats would be at night. She had been wondering if Aunt Annabelle might let them sleep out on the ridge, so they could listen until midnight or after. But she did not dare to speak of such a plan now—not after seeing a ghost walk right out here to the ridge. No matter what they might say, it still seemed as if that queer old man *must* have been a ghost. There just was not any other way to explain him.

There was so much watching and waiting to do in the days that followed that they thought the time would never end. They helped Aunt Annabelle around the house each morning and went up to Mr. Grant's and fed his hens. In the afternoons they stayed out in the pasture, listening beside the different rocks. During the evenings they stayed near the house in case Mr. Jarrett should return.

If they could have gone peacefully to bed when the long days of waiting were over, it would not have been so bad. But they had to keep awake and watch until midnight at Janice's window for the strange old man with the lantern. That was the most tiresome job of all.

Three warm, sunshiny days passed slowly by, with nothing happening at all. The children grew heavy-eyed and droopy from lack of sleep, and the excitement and fun seemed to have disappeared completely from their adventure.

On the fourth morning Aunt Annabelle asked the boys to trim the bushes around the front porch, so Janice said she would go up and feed Mr. Grant's hens.

The morning, though bright and sunny, was cold for July, and it felt good to set off up the road at a brisk pace. The hens began making loud, cackling noises when they heard her come up the driveway, and she knew they must be hungry. They were used to being fed early when Mr. Grant was at home.

"I'll give them plenty of grain this morning," she told herself, "to make up for being late."

She filled a big wooden measure and took it into the hen house where she filled the feeding troughs. The hens began tripping over each other and crowding around her to get at the food. Janice laughed as she watched them.

When they had quieted down, she was startled to hear a strange, hoarse cry almost in her ears.

"Marn-jay! Marn-jay!"

Looking up, she saw Blackie perched on a fence post, staring wickedly at her with his bright eyes. She

opened her hand, in which some of the chickens' grain remained.

"Come on, Blackie," she coaxed. "Come and get it."

To her delight the crow flew straight into the hen yard, perched on her shoulder, and began to nibble hungrily from her hand. When he had finished he flew back to the fence post and sat there watching her.

"Are you waiting for more, Blackie?" she asked.

She pumped water for the hens and then took another handful of grain and invited Blackie to come and eat from her hand again. This time she was outside the hen yard, and as the big bird perched on her shoulder and pecked at the grain she offered him, she began to walk down the driveway. Would he stay with her, she wondered? Could she get him home?

"You must be lost, Blackie," she told him. "Somebody must want you back again. You stay with me, and maybe I can help you find your home."

It was a strangely happy feeling to have the bird cling to her shoulder and to feel his smooth feathers against her hair. Once in a while he seemed to be trying to answer her talk with hoarse words of his own that she could not understand.

She moved more and more carefully as they drew close to Mountain View House, hardly daring to breathe for fear he would fly away. But Blackie seemed to have no desire to leave her. His bright eyes gazed at her trustingly now, without the curious, questioning look they had had at first.

Hubert and Tommy stared in openmouthed surprise when they saw her coming with the bird on her shoulder. They did not shout, though, but moved quietly toward her. Janice watched them come and wondered if Blackie would fly away now.

"I'm going to lose him, after all," she thought, feeling his claws dig more sharply into her shoulder as if getting ready for a take-off. But he did not fly. Instead, to her secret delight, he cuddled closer into her neck, his trembling body pressed against her hair. She reached up one hand to hold him, as she told the boys where she had found him.

They were standing on the lawn talking to Blackie and admiring him when Fred Reay, the mailman, pulled up beside the box at the foot of the driveway. He leaned his head out and shouted, "Hey! Where'd you find Pepette?"

"Pepette?" Hubert called back in bewilderment. "Who's Pepette?"

"Why—that crow you've got there. Did you find him? If you did, he must be Joe Boudreau's pet crow. The old man's been hunting for him for weeks now. He'll be real glad to have him back."

Janice held the bird closer than ever while the boys rushed over to talk with Fred. They learned that Joe

Boudreau was an old French-Canadian who lived alone on a dirt road that turned off the main road about a quarter of a mile toward town.

"He's a nice old fellow," Mr. Reay added, as he started to drive on. "Lonesome, though, since his wife died a few years ago. You'll be doing him a real kindness if you can get his bird back to him."

When he had gone the children began to plan what should be done. Aunt Annabelle came out and they told her about it.

"I think you should run along right now, while Blackie—or Pepette—or whatever his name is—is content to stay on Janice's shoulder," she said. "This will give us a chance to get acquainted with another of our neighbors, and that's fine."

CHAPTER 9

Two Mysteries Explained

The summer traffic was heavy, and the big cars flashing past them frightened Pepette so that Janice had to cuddle him in her arms. It was hard to believe that miles of wilderness surrounded them in every direction when there were so many gaily colored cars full of people passing them on the road.

Loneliness closed around them, though, when they left the highway and turned into a narrow lane among dark spruce trees. The day had continued to be chilly and in the shady places it was really cold. Two young fawns who were drinking from a brook near the road fled into the underbrush as the children approached.

"This is a queer place for anyone to live," Janice murmured. "If old Mr. Boudreau lives alone on this road he must be practically a hermit."

Just then they rounded a curve and saw cleared fields ahead of them, with a sagging barn and a weathered gray house close to the road. Was this Pepette's home?

They stopped a minute, gazing curiously at the solitary buildings. Suddenly Janice clutched Tommy's arm and said in a frightened whisper, "Look!"

An old man wearing a cap and a loose coat was walking slowly from the barn toward the house. He was bent with age, and carried a pail—instead of a smoky lantern—in one hand.

"It's the ghost!" Hubert exclaimed, his eyes staring in disbelief at the old man.

At that moment, with a hoarse cry and a terrific flapping of wings, Pepette sailed out of Janice's arms, flew straight over the fields to the old man, and settled in his arms.

"It's just—Joe Boudreau," Tommy muttered finally. "He must have been our ghost. Maybe now we can find out why he came to our house that night."

Mr. Boudreau had seen them and he hurried as fast as he was able around the side of the house toward them. Pepette sat on his shoulder and talked loudly and steadily as if he were explaining everything.

"You bring back my Pepette?" the old man asked, when they met at the end of his driveway. "I mus' thank you very much. I am so happy to have him back. How is it you find him?"

They all sat down on the front steps, and Janice poured out the story of how the bird had visited her on the pasture ridge and how she had fed him when she fed Mr. Grant's hens.

Joe Boudreau laughed. "Always he is hungry, my Pepette." He pointed a finger into the bird's saucy face and asked sternly, "Why you not come home? You know I hunt for you everywhere. You are very bad boy to scare poor Joe like that."

"Why *did* he stay away?" Tommy asked curiously. "You'd think he'd have come home when he got hungry. After all, he was never very far from here."

Joe Boudreau pointed to a tiger cat who was curled up in a patch of sun, sound asleep.

"That is Julie—you see? Julie came to me one night las' April. She is lost and very thin and hungry. So I think I take her in and keep her. But Pepette, he is jealous. He does not like Julie to stay here. He scold an' scold. Then at las' he fly away. First he stay only one night. Then he is gone two, three night. Finally he does not come home at all. When the storm comes up in the night, I go look for him—"

The old man broke off at an exclamation from the children.

"So it *was* you!" Janice gasped. "Oh, I'm so glad. We were so afraid you were a ghost."

Mr. Boudreau looked so puzzled Hubert hastened to explain about the fright he had given them on that stormy night.

The old man slapped his forehead in a gesture of despair. "Oh, my, oh, my, I am so sor-ree!" he cried.

"I think to myself, 'Nobody is awake in the old Totman house, so I just go out on the ridge to call Pepette.' He used to go to the old pasture there many times. The high wind and storm always scare my Pepette, so I think maybe he would come if he hear me call."

The children chattered excitedly until finally they and their new friend had the whole story straightened out.

"What does Pepette mean when he says 'Marn-jay —Marn-jay?' " Janice asked curiously.

Mr. Boudreau smiled. "I tol' you he is always hungry!" he said. "Man-ger—that is French word that means to eat."

The children burst into laughter. "So that's why we couldn't understand him. Pepette speaks French!"

They got up to go, and Tommy said happily, "Well, we've learned the answer to two mysteries this morning. We've found out who Pepette is and who the ghost was. Thank goodness we won't have to sit up till midnight tonight watching for anything."

Hubert stopped suddenly. "Mr. Boudreau, have you lived here very many years?" he asked.

"Many year!" the old man exclaimed. "But yes—I should say so. Nearly sixty year I live on this farm. I am twenty years old when I get married and come here from Canada. Oh, yes, I have live' here very long time."

"Did you ever hear the story people tell about a rock in our pasture that is supposed to be haunted?" Hubert asked excitedly. "The one where people used to hear the sound of galloping hoofs?"

Joe Boudreau nodded. "Oh, yes—that ghos' rock —I know him well."

"You do!" the children exclaimed.

"Oh, yes. I go there with my friends when I am young man. We never hear anything, but we talk with two, three people who have hear' the hoofbeats, so we get excited about them."

"Could you tell us which rock it is?" Hubert asked breathlessly.

"The biggest rock in the pasture—almost on top of the ridge—he is the one. Big gray rock, flat on top. You find him easy."

"Oh, thank you," Janice cried. "I know just which rock you mean. It's the one I chose the first time we went to the pasture to listen. Now we may be able to hear the hoofbeats."

Their old neighbor shook his head and gazed at them with a look of warning.

"Nobody hears the hoofbeats now," he said. "Maybe nothing is wrong with the old Totman house any more. That is all very old story. Better you should forget about it."

They thanked him again and said good-by. He urged them to come often and visit him and Pepette.

As they turned into the road he called after them, "Remember—is no use to hunt for trouble. This ghost has been quiet for a long time. Better you should let him be."

CHAPTER 10

Night on the Ridge

Now that they knew which rock was the right one, the children could not wait to get back to it. They fairly flew up their road and out to the pasture. When they reached the rock they stood still, just staring at it.

"Ghost rock!" Janice whispered, touching it with the palm of her hand. "At last we've found it. Now I'll believe that anything can happen."

"Now that we know we aren't wasting time in the wrong places, we can keep watch over this rock from morning to night," said Hubert.

"We ought to find a cubbyhole under the rock where we could keep books and paints and whittling wood," Tommy suggested. "Then we wouldn't grow tired sitting around here in all our spare time."

"Oh, that's a good idea," said Janice. "Let's look for a hiding place right now."

They began to pry around under the edges of the rock for a crevice or hole that might do. At last Tommy discovered a spot where three broken-off pieces of rock were lodged together to form a nook almost two feet wide. Juniper bushes and the overhanging rock sheltered the opening, too. They cleared it out and leveled off the dirt until they had a fine hiding place.

After lunch they brought their books, paints, and wood there and tucked them away. Janice even brought a jar of cookies so she could feed Pepette if he ever came back again.

All the rest of that day and evening they hovered close to the rock, and all the next day, too. Janice painted several water colors of the woods and mountains to send in letters to her friends back home. Several times, toward dusk, they saw deer come out of the woods and feed on the long grass at the pasture's edge. Tommy began a wood carving of a deer, and Hubert, who was more interested in skunks than any other animals, began to whittle one from one of Tommy's blocks of wood.

On the second evening, when it had grown nearly dark, Janice said decidedly, "We ought to stay out here all night. I still think it's in the night that we'd be likely to hear those hoofbeats."

96

"Do you think Aunt Annabelle would let us, Hubert?" asked Tommy. "I've always wanted to sleep out. It would be wonderful here, so close to the real big woods."

"Let's ask her!" they shouted together, and started for the house at a run.

Aunt Annabelle didn't think very highly of the idea.

"The mosquitoes would eat you alive before morning," she said. "And what if it should rain?"

"We can always come back to the house," Janice answered. "We'll be so near."

"But you might get frightened," she protested. "What if a bear or a wildcat came out of the woods?"

"My book about American wild animals says they never bother people unless you corner them or frighten them," said Hubert. "We'd be so near the house I don't believe any bears or wildcats would come."

At last Aunt Annabelle gave in.

"But I don't believe you'll stay all night," she declared. "I'll leave the kitchen door open, and unless I miss my guess you'll be back in your own beds by midnight."

She helped them collect old blankets and pillows, mosquito oil, flashlights, and a Thermos bottle of water. It was really dark when they started back to the ridge. They had to use their flashlights to find the path through the orchard and to pick out the most level place near the big rock to spread their blankets on.

"How black it is!" Janice exclaimed, when she had settled herself on her hard bed. "Not a single light except the stars and the fireflies."

"I don't care," said Tommy. "The only thing that really scared me was that old man with the lantern. No matter how hard I tried to believe there weren't any ghosts, I couldn't help thinking he must have been one. I couldn't think of any reason for an old man walking out here on a stormy midnight. But now that we've found an explanation for that, I don't feel scared of anything. Even if the hoofbeats should sound, I won't believe it's a ghost."

"I don't *think* I'll be afraid if we hear them," Janice said, "but it's bound to be very spooky, especially at night."

They did not talk very much. The deep silence around them was broken now and then by the chirping of insects in the grass, the late, sleepy sounds of birds, and even a distant loud calling, almost like a cow's mooing, that Hubert said was a moose.

Janice loved looking straight up into the starry sky. The Milky Way was a blurred white path across the arc of the heavens, and there was a quarter-moon dipping toward the west. The falling dew brought out the smell of the pines and fir trees more strongly, until the air was heavy with it.

"I'd like to sleep out all summer long," she said half to herself.

"So would I," Hubert answered promptly. "Maybe we could build a lean-to here and really camp out."

He and Tommy got so much interested in that plan that they sat up and talked about it until Janice was almost asleep.

But sleep did not come easily. She would feel herself drifting off into a comfortable doze, and then she would turn part way over and feel something hard pressing against her hip or her shoulder. After a while it would bother her so much she would have to throw off her blankets, find the lumpy place, and move to a better spot. Then it was hard to settle back again.

Sleep was fitful for them all. They dozed and woke and dozed and woke again, but they did not mind. The little cat naps refreshed them, and in between times it was thrilling to watch the quarter-moon set behind the western mountains and the stars grow bigger and brighter in the sky.

Finally, when they had given up the idea of getting a real night's sleep, they all sank into slumber. The night sounds went on around them, an owl cried in the woods, and the stars continued their march across the sky, but the three children were lost in dreams.

Janice woke suddenly and sharply from a dream that someone was pounding on her door. She half sat up and mumbled "Yes, yes. I'm coming."

Then, as she realized where she was, her heart stood still. That was no knocking on her door. The sound that had wakened her came again. *Click-click! Clickety-click!* Loud and fast it came from the big rock that loomed up in the darkness beside her. *The hoofbeats were galloping in the ghost rock, at last!*

For a minute she could not make a sound. When she opened her mouth and tried to call Tommy, her voice stuck in her throat. Shivers were running over her, and she felt as if she were in the middle of a nightmare.

She got out a choked cry after a minute, and Tommy and Hubert woke instantly. They did not have to ask what was the matter. The clear, ringing *clickety-click* sounded as loud on the night air as if the horse were galloping right beside them. It could not be a real horse, and neither could it be a ghost. So what was it?

Hubert turned his flashlight full upon the rock. There it stood, gray and bare as always. He flashed the beam around the pasture in every direction, but there was nothing to be seen.

As suddenly as the hoofbeats had begun, they stopped. Even then, the children held their breath, waiting. Would the—creature—gallop again? They sat in shivering silence, frightened and wondering.

After a little while Tommy said in a shaky voice, "Well, at least we didn't run!"

"I wanted to," Janice admitted, "but I was too scared to move. I'm still scared."

"I'm not," declared Hubert, his voice ringing out boldly in the darkness. "I admit that sound was spooky, and it made me shiver for a few minutes. But I'm not afraid any more. I'm glad. Now we know it's true, and Mr. Grant will pay attention to our story."

"He ought to be able to do something about it," Tommy said. "The men in the Border Patrol must have plenty of mysteries more serious than this to figure out."

"He'll be home tomorrow," Janice reminded them. "I just can't wait to tell him everything that's happened."

Nobody could think of sleep, for they were much too excited. Now that the rock was quiet again, they could hardly believe they had really heard the weird sounds coming from it. They exclaimed over and over about how real the hoofbeats had been. Surely they could not have been made by anything else but a real horse galloping.

"Or a ghost horse," Janice murmured in a small voice, "if anybody believed in ghosts."

They went over the story Mr. Grant had told them, and all the happenings in between, trying to figure out the meaning of it all. They talked and talked until at last the sky began to glow with a rosy light behind Boundary-Bald, and they knew that morning was not far away.

CHAPTER 11

But Not After Midnight!

Aunt Annabelle had a big breakfast ready for them when they got back to the house.

"You did very well to stay out all night," she said warmly. "You've proved that you're real campers."

As they chattered about their experiences watching the stars and hearing the moose call off in the distance, they wondered what she would say if they told her about the pounding hoofbeats in the rock.

"Mr. Jarrett came again last night," she told them, after a minute. "He left very early this morning, for some reason. It was lucky I had that third-floor room ready for him."

The children laid down their forks and stared at each other, speechless. Even the thrill of hearing the hoofbeats was forgotten for the moment. Mr. Jarrett had come—and gone—and they had missed him.

Had he used his light and searched the top floor again?

"I have to do some shopping in Jackman this morning," Aunt Annabelle went on. "Do you want to go with me and have a swim in the lake?"

"I guess not," Janice answered quickly, with a meaningful glance at the boys. "We've got some things to do around here."

The boys understood her look. How lucky it would be if they could be left alone this morning! They could look in Mr. Jarrett's room and the hiding place on the third floor, and they could wait for Mr. Grant. If he came while Aunt Annabelle was gone, they'd have a chance to tell him about Joe Boudreau and Pepette, and Mr. Jarrett, and the hoofbeats in the rock, and everything!

"We don't feel like swimming this morning," Hubert declared. "Tommy and I are going to build a lean-to in the pasture and we—we want to get started on it."

"Huh," sniffed Aunt Annabelle. "That's the first time I ever knew you to pass up a chance for a swim. But I suppose you've got camping fever now and won't rest until you get your lean-to built."

As soon as she departed for Jackman the children rushed up to the third floor and into the corner room closet. Tommy had his jackknife, and it took only a few seconds to pry up the loose board. But their haste and excitement had been needless, for they found everything exactly as it had been before.

"Shucks," said Tommy, backing out of the closet and dusting his hands, "just that same old flashlight."

But Hubert's eyes had a strange gleam in them. "How dumb can we be?" he gasped, plunging back into the closet and lifting up the board again. "This may be a signal light. Maybe Mr. Jarrett wanted a room on this top floor because he wanted to signal to somebody with this light!"

"I bet you're right, Hubert," Tommy exclaimed. "It's a very powerful light. It could be seen for miles from this high window up here."

They went to the window and looked out. Endless acres of forest were all that could be seen, stretching off to the mountains along the border.

"Who could he be signaling to—out there?" Janice asked doubtfully.

Tommy's blue eyes and Hubert's dark ones met, and the same look flashed into them both.

"Smugglers! That's who he might signal to. And we've got to tell Mr. Grant," they cried, starting for the stairs.

This time they did not have long to wait. They had hardly reached the back door when Mr. Grant drove into the yard. He swung the car to a stop and leaped out with an eager smile, as the children rushed up to him.

"Hi!" he called. "I thought I'd stop in and see my neighbors before I went home. It's almost like having a family of my own, having you people to come back to!"

Even in her excitement, Janice couldn't help feeling proud at his words. He looked browner and more handsome than ever after his week in the woods.

"Oh, Mr. Grant," she said, taking him by the arm and leading him to the front steps. "Sit down. We're so glad to see you, and we've got so much to tell you!"

"Yes," Hubert and Tommy half shouted. "We think Mr. Jarrett has been signaling to the smugglers. And we thought we saw a ghost, only it was just Joe Boudreau. And we found Pepette—and we heard the hoofbeats—"

"Hey!" interrupted their neighbor, with a protesting laugh. "Wait a minute here. You're going too fast for me. I think you'd better start at the beginning. What's this about Joe Boudreau? And who's Pepette?"

They all began to talk at once, telling the story of the old man with his lantern and how they had thought it *must* be the ghost of the Totmans' hired man, only it turned out to be old Joe Boudreau.

"Well, for Pete's sake!" Mr. Grant exclaimed. "What was Joe doing in your back yard on a stormy midnight?"

Hubert told the rest of the story about Pepette. Mr. Grant listened with interest, but Janice thought his attention roved a little. He kept turning his head toward the house, and when Hubert had barely finished the story he interrupted as if he had not really been listening.

"Er—that's good, kids. I'm certainly glad you found old Joe's pet. But say—where's Mrs. Lewis this morning? I'd like to say hello to her, too."

Janice said to herself in sudden surprise, "Mr. Grant likes Aunt Annabelle! He's more interested in seeing her than he is in our story!"

She pushed that romantic thought away for a moment while she explained where Aunt Annabelle was, and assured him that she would be back soon.

"But Mr. Grant," she continued, "we've got something even more important to tell you. Mr. Boudreau told us how to find the ghost rock, and—"

"And last night we heard the hoofbeats in the rock!" Tommy and Hubert shouted, finishing the story for her in one breath.

Mr. Grant opened his eyes wide in amazement. "You *did!* You really heard them? Well—great Scott! You're the first people to hear those hoofbeats for thirty years or more!"

They waited, rather proudly, for his first amazement to subside. Then Hubert said pointedly, "Now we've got to find out what's causing them, you know. You told us it couldn't be a ghost—and we promised not to tell Mom about them—but Mr. Grant, we've just *got* to prove that there isn't a curse on this house."

Mr. Grant, whose eyes had been following the progress of the cars along the road as if he expected Aunt Annabelle to return at any minute, forced his attention back to their story.

"Well now, look here," he said seriously, "we don't any of us believe there really is a curse on Mountain View House, do we? I thought you understood that that was just a story."

"Some people believe it," Hubert declared stubbornly. "The boy who brings the milk believes it. He leaves the bottles beside the mailbox every day because he doesn't like to come up to this house. And one of the electricians believes it—he wouldn't come here to fix the sign." .

"Oh, Mr. Grant," Janice pleaded, "you *will* help us, won't you? Aunt Annabelle will be all alone here in the winter, and we want to feel safe about her."

"Great Scott!" their friend exclaimed again. "I had no idea you were so serious about all those old stories I told you. I'm perfectly certain that even if the hoofbeats really do sound in the rock—and I never quite believed they did, before—there's some natural explanation of the sound. I used to hear people discussing it years ago. They always agreed that if there really were hoofbeats in that rock, they must have been caused by vibrations in the ridge underneath it. They had it figured out that a horse somewhere —maybe at some lumber camp—was galloping along where that same ridge runs through the forest, and the vibrations carried for miles along it and sort of echoed in that particular rock."

For a moment that explanation seemed reasonable to the children. After all, the old man with the lantern had not been a ghost, and Pepette had not been a mysterious visitor from the wilderness. Other people who stayed at Mountain View House lately had not had anything happen to them. And the ghostly hoofbeats in the rock were nothing to be excited about—just vibrations and echoes.

But Janice could still hear that clear, ringing, ghostly *click-click* in her ears. Surely there was something more than what Mr. Grant had said. Why did they come only at midnight—or after? Horses were working in the woods all day, yet they never made the sounds in the rock then.

"Mr. Grant," she said solemnly, "I think you must be wrong. It was late last night that we heard those hoofbeats. Horses at the lumber camps might gallop through the woods in the daytime. *But not after midnight.* Why would work horses in a lumber camp be galloping around the woods in the middle of the night?"

Mr. Grant stared at her, and this time there was no

mistaking the complete, amazed attention he was giving to her words. His eyes had a keen, speculating look, and when he closed his mouth he looked grim. All in a moment he had stopped being just a gay, friendly neighbor. He had become wholly the Border Patrol man, as stern as the guns that bristled in his belt.

"Not after midnight, Janice, you're very right," he said at last, and his face relaxed for a second as he smiled at her. "And you're right, too, Hubert—this is something more serious than we had thought."

He got up and started toward his car, but the children caught his arms.

"You haven't heard about Mr. Jarrett yet—and the signal light," they told him.

He sat down again and listened while they told about the strange visitor who had insisted on a back room on the third floor, and who kept a flashlight hidden there.

"Show me the place," Mr. Grant directed briefly, when they had finished.

They led him to the corner room and showed him the powerful flashlight in its hiding place under the floor. He went to the window just as they had done and looked off over the miles of dense forests, as if marking the lay of the land.

"Look here, kids," he said seriously, as they went down the stairs. "Don't fool around with this mystery any more. Stay away from the pasture and this top-floor hiding place until you hear from me. You may have stumbled upon something pretty important—and dangerous, too. You'll hear from me soon, but in the meantime, stick close to home—and to Mrs. Lewis. And don't breathe a word of this to anyone. Okay?"

"Okay!" the children agreed.

"One more thing," he added. "If Mr. Jarrett comes again, will one of you come up to my house and let me know? If I'm not there, you can leave a couple of big stones on my doorstep. But don't hang around to wait for me, and don't say or do anything here at home to make the man suspect that you know what he's up to."

They nodded, and with a wave of the hand Mr. Grant drove away.

CHAPTER 12

The Pride of the Border Patrol

By the time Aunt Annabelle got home, the children were in such suspense they could hardly make sensible answers to her questions.

"How far did you get with your lean-to?" she asked when they were eating lunch.

"Lean-to?" Hubert repeated vacantly. "Lean-to? Oh-er-no, we didn't."

"No, you didn't," Aunt Annabelle echoed, her voice rising, "What kind of an answer is that?"

"He means we decided not to build one," Tommy said quickly.

"But why not?" she demanded. "When I left, you were all enthused about the idea."

It was as if they did not hear her. The three children, with their thoughts far away, went on eating their potato salad and cold ham.

"Did anything happen while I was gone?" Aunt Annabelle asked curiously.

There was no answer to that question, either, for a minute, and she repeated it in a louder tone, tacking Janice's name firmly to the end of the question.

Janice started. "Oh—er—yes. Mr. Grant came while you were gone. He was sorry not to see you, but he had to leave again in quite a hurry."

Aunt Annabelle gave up.

"You're all so sleepy you don't know what you're saying," she declared. "I don't believe you got any sleep at all last night out there in the pasture."

That afternoon, wild speculations and ideas ran through the minds of the three children. The most puzzling problem was that there seemed to be two different mysteries, and Mr. Grant had seemed to be disturbed about them both. Surely Mr. Jarrett and his signal light could not have anything to do with the hoofbeats they had heard in the ghost rock, could they?

They were to puzzle over that problem for a much longer time than they had expected. Several days passed, and Mr. Grant did not come near. The children took walks and played croquet and basketball by the hour. They amazed Aunt Annabelle by suggesting jobs they could do around the house. Even with all that, time hung heavy on their hands.

Guests came and went quite regularly now, and this kept Aunt Annabelle as cheerful as a robin in the springtime. The children kept a watchful eye on all the people who came. Almost a week had passed when, one evening, the hard-eyed Mr. Jarrett appeared again. He drove into the yard just before dark and passed the children, who were having a game of tag on the lawn, without a word.

"Keep right on playing," Hubert said in a low voice, as he tagged Janice and ran toward Tommy. "Don't let him think we've noticed him at all."

They kept on with their game until Mr. Jarrett had had time to speak to Aunt Annabelle and go to his room. Then they whispered together for a minute in the shadow of the big maple tree.

"Only one of us should go to Mr. Grant's," Tommy said. "If Mr. Jarrett should notice that none of us were around it might make him suspect something."

"I'll go," Hubert offered promptly. "If Mr. Grant isn't there, I'll leave some stones on his doorstep the way he told us to do, and hurry right back. You keep on playing out here, and nobody will know I've gone."

He started up the road at a run. Tommy and Janice were glad it was so nearly dark that he could hardly be seen. No one paid any attention to them as they went on playing tag and shouting back and forth. They kept it up until they were out of breath and darkness had settled over everything.

Hubert came puffing into the yard just as they heard Aunt Annabelle calling that it was time to come in.

"He wasn't there," Hubert whispered, "but I left the stones, so he'll know."

They thought it would be impossible to sleep a wink that night, with Mr. Jarrett prowling around the top floor in the darkness and all kinds of exciting things likely to happen, but they did. They slept so soundly they did not even hear any footsteps.

In the morning, when it seemed as if they really would die of impatience and curiosity, Mr. Grant's car swung into the driveway, and he leaped out and strode into the kitchen where they were all helping Aunt Annabelle shell peas.

"Well," exclaimed Aunt Annabelle, jumping up to shake hands with him, "am I glad to see you! These children have been like lost souls ever since you were here a few days ago. Now maybe you'll tell me what's been going on around here."

Mr. Grant straddled a kitchen chair and rested his arms across the back of it. He cleared his throat a little nervously.

"It's a long story, Mrs. Lewis," he began, "and you may feel I started these children on a dangerous adventure by the stories I foolishly told them when we first met. But I assure you I never dreamed of anything coming of it. And before I explain anything, I want to tell you that right this minute your children are heroes here in Jackman. They're the pride of the Border Patrol this morning!"

Janice, Tommy, and Hubert stared at him. "We *are!*" Janice gasped. "Oh, tell us about it!"

"Just give me a couple of minutes to explain the first part of the story to Mrs. Lewis," he said, "then I'll tell you every single thing."

He turned to Aunt Annabelle and repeated the story he had told the children about the things that had happened at Mountain View House, and how people had come to believe there was a curse on the place.

Aunt Annabelle shivered. "So that's why even the milkman doesn't want to come in!" she said.

"I always thought it was a lot of nonsense, except for the sound of the hoofbeats in the rock," Mr. Grant said. "So many respectable people claimed to have heard them, in the past, it was hard to deny that that part of the story might be true. But most of us thought it was probably caused by something very natural— such as a continuation of the long, rocky ridge into the forest, where a work horse from one of the lumber camps might gallop across it and set vibrations going that echoed in the rock."

"That sounds reasonable," Aunt Annabelle nodded.

"But I suppose these youngsters couldn't rest until they heard the hoofbeats for themselves. And now I understand why they spent all their time out on the ridge!"

"Luckily for all of us," Mr. Grant said quickly, "they wanted to help you. They wanted to prove that there was nothing ghostly about the hoofbeats. In their efforts to clear up the mystery surrounding Mountain View House they unexpectedly came upon the answer to a much more dangerous mystery."

"Oh, Mr. Grant, what was it?" Tommy cried, leaning toward him with shining, eager eyes.

"Do you remember my telling you about the trouble we've been having with aliens being smuggled across the border here the past year or two?" Mr. Grant asked.

They nodded, their eyes fixed upon his face.

"Well—we had tried every way we could think of to find out about this smuggling. We stopped the trains and buses and searched them. We visited the lumber camps on sudden surprise visits. We patrolled the woods along the border more thoroughly than we've ever patrolled them before. We were suspicious of outsiders who came to town, and we even kept an eye on workers who'd been here for years who seemed to have more money to spend on fancy cars and luxuries than they'd had before. But we discovered nothing. We couldn't seem to find a clue anywhere. It was making things uncomfortable for us here in the patrol, you can believe."

"And the hoofbeats were a clue?" Janice asked breathlessly.

"The hoofbeats were a clue," Mr. Grant repeated solemnly. "They were more than a clue. They were the key that unlocked the whole problem."

"But how?" Hubert demanded.

"Well," Mr. Grant continued, "there were a couple of new outfits who came into the woods to operate logging camps here two years ago. That wasn't unusual, except that they were outsiders we'd never dealt with before, not working for any of the big lumber companies. We kept quite a watch on them. Sometimes we'd drop in on them unexpectedly around ten o'clock at night and check on the men. Everything was always okay.

"But after we heard about the hoofbeats, we began to think. Could somebody be running people across the border on horseback in the middle of the night? Horses traveling one of the woods trails wouldn't make much noise, and besides, we didn't often patrol the woods after midnight.

"So we followed the ridge into the woods for several miles. We discovered a trail, recently traveled, that crossed the ridge at a hard, rocky spot. It must have been from there that the hoofbeats carried to the rock where you children heard them."

He paused a minute to explain to Aunt Annabelle about Mr. Jarrett and his part in the mystery.

"When the children showed me that powerful flashlight hidden on the top floor of this house, I realized the smugglers must wait for a signal from Jarrett before finishing the last lap of the trail—from a lumber camp not far from here to a private car that would be waiting on the road nearby.

"So when the children left word for me that Jarrett was here last night, we hid out along the trail and captured our men. The two lumber camps were a bluff to cover the operations of a gang who were making a fortune out of smuggling aliens into the United States. Thanks to these three children we caught them red-handed and were able to arrest them all. Jarrett, too. We followed him when he left here this morning and arrested him when he stopped in Jackman for gas."

He turned apologetically to Aunt Annabelle. "I'm sure you know I would never have told those old stories to the children if I'd had any idea there was anything so dangerous connected with them."

Aunt Annabelle smiled at him warmly. "Why, of course I understand," she said. "And I'm glad it turned out so well. I'm proud of Janice and Tommy and Hubert. I know they're delighted to have been of help to you and the patrol."

"And you're not worried because of the ghost rock

and all those old stories about the house?" Janice asked.

"Goodness no," Aunt Annabelle said. "I think it's wonderful. People would love to stop at a haunted house. It would be grand for business. Maybe we could change the name of the house. We could call it 'Ghost Rock House.' I bet people would like that!"

Mr. Grant shook his head, as if Aunt Annabelle were a naughty child carried away with an exciting plan.

"You've got to remember this is a frontier region, Mrs. Lewis, and some of the dangers are no joke. Even with the ghost rock mystery cleared up, it's still lonely country for a woman. A place like this needs a man."

Then his face turned scarlet and so did Aunt Annabelle's. He spoke to the children hastily.

"Anyway, kids, tomorrow the men of the Border Patrol want to take you out to dinner. The chief patrol inspector in Maine has heard the story and he's coming to the dinner all the way from Houlton to thank you in person. The other fellows in the patrol here wanted me to find out if there was anything in particular that you'd like to have them do for you."

Tommy and Hubert were so dazzled by the prospect of being honored by the chief of the Border Patrol they could not think of anything else, but Janice spoke up a little timidly.

"Do you think we could have our pictures taken with all the men in their uniforms?"

"You certainly could," Mr. Grant promised.

When he had gone the children were in such a state of excitement they could hardly eat their lunch. Afterward, Aunt Annabelle insisted that they must get letter paper and write the entire story to Janice and Tommy's mother and father back home.

"They'll be proud of you, too," she said. "It's a shame they couldn't be here tomorrow to see you off to your dinner with the Border Patrol."

As they sat on the porch writing their letters Janice looked dreamily off at the mountains that ringed them round. Boundary-Bald was clear blue in the sunlight, the fire tower on its summit plainly visible against the sky. Today it seemed like an old friend standing guard over Mountain View House and the people in it.

"I love Boundary-Bald," she said happily. "It's the most beautiful thing in all this beautiful country. I'm going to miss it awfully when we go back home."

The dinner next day was the most exciting and satisfying occasion the children had ever known. They had steaks and strawberry shortcake, and the men drank a toast to the children who had helped them solve their most difficult problem. The chief made a short speech, and everyone in the hotel dining room cheered. Afterward, when they went outside to have

·their picture taken, it seemed to Janice the proudest moment of her life.

When it was all over, it was fun to settle down again to just enjoying the pleasant summer days, with no ghost stories to worry them. Hubert and Tommy finished their lean-to, and they all camped out in it often.

Mr. Grant came almost every day or evening, and the children were delighted when, near the end of the summer, he and Aunt Annabelle announced that they were going to be married in the fall, if the children did not mind.

Hubert rose proudly to the occasion.

"Mind?" he asked in amazement. "Why, this is the best thing that's *ever* happened. This is even better than being honored by the Border Patrol, because this makes us all *related* to it!"

"With a man in the house, and beautiful Boundary-Bald so near to keep guard over it, nobody's ever going to have to worry about Aunt Annabelle again," Janice murmured dreamily.